Brumbletide
and the Golden Blood Warmouth

🕯 J. Reese Bradley 🕯

Copyright © 2024 by J Reese Bradley

Illustrations copyright © 2024 Brynn Miller

All rights reserved. This book or any portion thereof may not be reproduced or used in any manner whatsoever without the express written permission of the publisher except for the use of brief quotations in a book review.

Printed in the United States of America

To the LORD Jesus Christ,
the King above all kings,
to whom Pippin, Aslan,
and all the rest bow and glorify.

Table of Contents

Chapter 1 Has Anyone Seen the Digglewip? 1
Chapter 2 The Little Ipswich Library 2
Chapter 3 Miss Squaffletree is Safe 11
Chapter 4 Remember, Maggie 19
Chapter 5 Rexes and Reginas 27
Chapter 6 Heated Thoughts 39
Chapter 7 Mind's Eye 47
Chapter 8 Whitescales 55
Chapter 9 Verecundiam 61
Chapter 10 Hoplology Happenings 69
Chapter 11 The Messenger 74
Chapter 12 Doomed 81
Chapter 13 Clair Shelley 87
Chapter 14 I Believe You 95
Chapter 15 Funny Haha 101
Chapter 16 The Eyes in the Wall 107
Chapter 17 Useless, Stupid, Failure 122
Chapter 18 The Treehouse Deer 130
Chapter 19 Another Dragon 139
Chapter 20 The Golden Blood Warmouth 149
Chapter 21 Marked 161
Chapter 22 Legends 171
Chapter 23 Boggletrice for Pippin 183
Chapter 24 The Eighth Door 190
Chapter 25 Blood for Blood 197

Chapter 1
Has Anyone Seen the Digglewip?

W here did it go? I cannot, for the life of me, remember what happened to the Digglewip. The last I saw the magical map was at the Changing of the Crowns ceremony. Not the big Changing of the Crowns in the Throne Room where the Six almost died of old age, but the small Changing of the Crowns ceremony that happened on the ferry with only Gus, Mrs. Cloudt, the Horsemen, and my friends. Thorn was there too. It was there that I was made Head Queen of Emily Castle, and it was there that I last saw the Digglewip. Since most everyone on the ferry that day is here in this cottage, it makes sense that one of the Boggletrice Company would have it.

The Boggletrice Company consists of Gus, the lovable bartender and owner of The Lazy Jug, Mrs. Cloudt, the baker of Downtown Ipswich, and the Horsemen, who are three undercover royals that used to be attendants for Emily's ferry. Each of the

Horsemen transforms into horse-people with the power of the Scepter of the Seven. Also a member of the Company is the ever-elusive King McShanihan, who drifted in as a very mysterious Head of Emily Academy for a short time. His true identity was hidden with the help of his magical coronet, which seems to have a mind of its own and is named Aquila. Lastly is Jericho, a friendly and soft-spoken Snickerling who was a spy in the castle for Pippin's six remaining Chosen: Justice, George, Flori, Sara Lisa, Eve, and Soleil.

We have all just finished dinner and are getting ready to settle in for the night. I take a cup of Bubblegin, eyeing Gus. Does Gus by chance have the Digglewip? Along with being the bartender of the pub, Gus also happens to be a descendant of Queen Sara Lisa of Fairfang and her estranged husband, Boris, who isn't actually estranged at all but is now Ignatius, the talking fire of Emily. As of now, Sara Lisa still doesn't know that Ignatius is Boris, but many secrets are being revealed lately, so I'm sure it's only a matter of time. Where would Gus keep it if he did have the map? In here, the Boggletrice Company headquarters? Or is it on the other side of the fireplace in the pub?

What about Mrs. Cloudt? Would the sweet little old lady be keeping it because she is so unsuspecting? Would she keep it in her bakery a few doors down? It has been closed for weeks since Gus and Martha have been busy helping the ancestors and the rest of us hide from the Einsreich. The Einsreich are a red-eyed, wicked zombie race of royal academy students that have infiltrated Castle Emily. They were somehow infused with warmouth blood at their home school, Infernum Militant Academy. They and Thorn's father, Tritch Anguis, and the headmaster of Infernum Militant Academy, King Klauschwitz, are why we are all in this secret cottage hidden from the castle and Little Ipswich. We, the Boggletrice Company, are gathering information and forming a plan to stop the Einsreich and defeat Tritch, Klauschwitz, and anyone else responsible for the killing of innocent Snickerlings for their magic.

McShanihan? Could King McShanihan have the Digglewip? He is definitely the most likely culprit, and if he does have it, then there is no telling where it is hiding. It could literally be anywhere around the world—maybe even my childhood treehouse that he has strangely taken a liking to.

How about the Horsemen? Could Anastasia, Henry, or Cornelius have it? Maybe on the ferry where I last saw it? That would be a problem because we can only go back to the castle once we are absolutely ready to fight the Einsreich.

I glance up at the ugly head on the wall that holds the Scepter of the Seven in its mouth. Maybe the map is in there? But I don't see anything behind the leather sack. Still, I will check when no one is looking if the opportunity arises.

Martha sets out the pillows and blankets for all of us to sleep on tonight. Fergus, the warmouth hound, and Zelda, the dragon, playfully tug at the blankets as she lays them down. "Oh, stop that. Bad boy. Bad girl. Get on now." Martha shoos them away, but the winged dog and dragon only hover with their tongues out, panting happily.

When everyone is up cleaning the table and tidying the cottage, curiosity finally gets the best of me. I slide in next to Soleil, who is washing dishes at the sink.

"Soleil?" I ask quietly.

"Yes, Princess?" she replies, drying a cup.

"Where has the Digglewip gone? I don't know what made me think of it, but it seems I haven't seen it in forever."

"Hmm, that's a good question. I don't know." And without warning, she turns and yells, "Everyone! Where is the Digglewip? Maggie wants to know."

My cheeks burn.

Justice replies, "I'm not sure. What do you want with it, Maggie?"

What do I want with it? "I just thought it could help us somehow?"

"She may be onto something," says George. "Where is the map?"

Ernie, who is new to everything, watches everyone curiously. This has all got to be quite a shock for him since he has been living all by himself on Dragon Street ever since accidentally starting a fire at his house that killed his whole family. But when all of the Boggletrice Company went out into Little Ipswich looking for anyone with Pippin's mark, Ernie was the *only* one who had it.

"Has anyone seen the Digglewip?" asks Cornelius, who is entirely human now. He and the other Horsemen could finally turn back from horse-people when we got the Scepter from McShanihan, who had been camping out in the treehouse Wes and I had made a few summers back.

The ancestors all deny having the magical map, and so do Lenore, Jericho, and my friends.

Gus had to go to the pub for something a minute ago, and Martha is in the kitchen making tea. Of everyone in the room, Gus and Martha are the least likely to have it. I bet McShanihan kept it—just like him to steal away items that would be useful to us in fighting Tritch Anguis and the Einsreich.

Why in the world would McShanihan, the most powerful of Pippin's Chosen, leave us to ourselves while he stays in our treehouse in the woods? And Pippin! Can't he put a stop to all of this at once? What on earth is he waiting for? Why is he having us risk our lives to fight for him if he thinks so much of us? What kind of plan is this? A ridiculous one if you ask me. Blimey! Calysta, Wes, Atticus—they almost died! I almost died when fighting Michelle. What kind of king has a thirteen-year-old fight the villain in his place?

The Boggletrice Company has settled back into talk of the weather and ailments until Soleil tells us all to get a good night's rest because she has ideas to share in the morning.

My thoughts circle back to the Digglewip. Where is it? I want to find it. Sure, it will be helpful in fighting the Einsreich, but my reason for wanting to see it is different from that of the rest of the Boggletrice Company. My reason for wanting the Digglewip is only to give it a glimpse. Just one single glance.

Because I do not think I will see anything on it.

Brynn Miller, age 12

Chapter 2
The Little Ipswich Library

Magnus, Eve's lovable flying pig, squeaks in my ear and nuzzles my nose to wake me up to the delightful smell of eggs, bacon, and coffee. Everyone else is just getting up too, even the warmouths who groggily fly over the pile of pillows and blankets. Martha and, surprisingly, Queen Lenore are the ones who've made the morning meal.

"Your Majesty," yawns Calysta to Lenore. "I didn't know you could cook. You certainly didn't need to in your position at Emily."

Lenore laughs. "You would be right, my dear, and I suggest you not expect too much from the eggs."

She wasn't joking. We all sit down to a meal of bacon that is somehow crispy and floppy at the same time and black scrambled eggs. Jack, a friend who also happens to give my stomach butterflies whenever he's around, picks up a crumpet.

"These look fine."

"Mrs. Cloudt made those," Lenore admits.

"Call me Martha," Mrs. Cloudt calls over her shoulder busily cleaning the kitchen.

Everyone is seated at the table eating breakfast except for Soleil. She stands with a mug of tea, waiting for everyone to get settled.

"Alright, Soleil, what you got?" asks George through a mouthful of food. "Gotta be better than these eggs."

Lenore's cheeks turn rosy. Never in a million years would I ever imagine Queen Lenore being embarrassed about anything.

"Be nice, George," scolds Sara Lisa. "You make the eggs next time."

"Yeah, yeah, what you got, Soleil?"

Soleil gleams. She takes a sip of her tea before speaking. "I've been pondering these Einsreich royals. They are infused with warmouth blood, so they must have been real children at one time. Or perhaps they *still* are real children inside the zombies. If I could get to my library, I could research warmouth blood and work on an antidote that would bring them back to normal."

"Stop right there," pipes George. "We cannot get attached to the idea that we can save those kids. Not only do we have no way of getting to your library, but we don't have time to wait for you to concoct an antidote—and we don't even know if it is, in fact, real children inside those demons."

"I've already been thinking of one that might work. I think I could be quick. But you're right. There's no way of getting to my books."

Wes perks up, "I'll take you to the Little Ipswich Library. They may not have the books you need, but you'll be blown away by what they do have."

Soleil grins. "Really? Alright, Prince Wesley, what do we have to lose?"

"I'm going with you guys. It's getting stuffy in here," I tell them.

"Oh, can I come too?" asks Calysta.

"Me too," adds Atticus.

George throws a hand. "Be fast. This isn't a group study with mates."

"We'll be back in a jiff," Soleil assures him.

"I'll stay behind this time. I'm starving. I'll eat whatever you guys don't." Jack is a brawny athletic boy who needs a lot of calories. I'm a little relieved he isn't coming.

"Do be careful. Keep watch around you at all times," says Eve from the armchair. Magnus is perched on her shoulder, and Teddy, the beaver, has gone back to sleep on her feet.

"We will," says Wes, zipping his jacket. "I know this place like the back of my hand."

This is true. Wes is obsessed with space and frequents the library for all the information on it he can possibly obtain. He has even badgered the librarian for years to get more books on the subject because he's read all the library's stock several times over.

Before we know what hit us, we are fed and up and stepping

through the fire on our way to the Little Ipswich Library.

"Hurry back, friends. It's trying times."

"We will, Ignatius," I tell the fire, having no feeling of assurance at all as usual.

Lazy Jug is empty at the early hour, but it won't be empty all day. Gus has opened the pub again to thwart any suspicion that something unusual is happening, so he will be working from noon to midnight. No one knows that the fire warming everyone in the February freeze is a portal to the secret hideaway of the Boggletrice Company, where a bunch of kings and queens, princes and princesses, and a slew of magical creatures are scheming Emily's demise. Gus is unstacking chairs when we all enter. "Top of the mornin'. Where we headin'?"

Wes explains everything to Gus. I glance around the pub for any hint of the Digglewip. In what seems like seconds, I haven't heard a word Wes said, but Gus is bidding us good luck and farewell.

The bell on the door jingles as we exit the pub. Wes, Calysta, Atticus, and I are all dressed in regular clothes but have our crowns on, which is probably stranger than Soleil's head-to-toe royal ensemble. We hurry down the cobblestone street in the direction of the library, but just three doors down, we meet someone who sends us all gasping and darting into the alleyway. Standing on the sidewalk in front of Cloudt's Bakery is yet another royal. She is tall, broad, and pale. Her eyes are red and distant. She is an Einsreich.

"Holy moly!" exclaims Wes.

"What's it doing outside the castle?" I breathe.

"Tritch Anguis must have sent them. Do you think they are looking for us?" whispers Calysta.

"I don't know. It had to have seen us," says Atticus. "Why didn't it scream or anything?"

"Your guess is as good as mine, young ones," says Soleil. "Let us not go that way. Is there a different way to the library?"

"Follow me," says Wes, leading us to the alley's other end. We poke our heads around the corner to the back of the shops. Two Einsreich boys are standing at the back of the pub and ice cream parlor.

"There's no way around it. We'll have to make a run for it," Wes whispers urgently. "On the count of three...."

We all take a deep breath. Wes is right. There's no other way.

"One," says Atticus.

"Two," I add.

"THREE!" we all say together, not quietly at all, as we rush out of the alley in the opposite direction of the Einsreich. We follow Wes as he speeds past the backdoors of the Downtown Ipswich shops. We are almost to the edge of town. The bridge isn't far. Will there be Einsreich at the bridge too? What do we do then?

We cross through another alleyway. The bridge is right ahead guarded by two Einsreich girls.

We halt, running into each other.

"What do we do?" asks Calysta.

"We can't go back," says Wes. "We have to try to run past them."

"Is there no other way?" pleads Soleil.

"There's no other way." Wes sounds so grown up.

"Let's go!" shouts Atticus, and we all sprint as fast as we can to the bridge past the Einsreich and into the town. The Einsreich didn't budge.

Panting, we slow down once we reach the Ipswich wall.

"What was that about? What are they doing?" I say between breaths.

"Seems like absolutely nothing, doesn't it?" says Atticus. "They're just standing there like gargoyles."

"Curious, indeed," says Soleil. "But we must make haste. Let us be on our way."

When we have all caught our breath a bit, we follow Wes a short distance to the library. I'd like to shake the hand of whoever decided to put the library *outside* of Downtown Ipswich.

The Ipswich Library is down a little side street by the wood, almost hidden. Wes may be correct that the Little Ipswich Library is "regular" in that you will find all the books your local library has and a media center for research and study, but it is not at all regular in its setup.

The unsuspecting dirt road becomes more and more elaborate as you go. The dirt road becomes gravel; the gravel becomes cobblestone. The cobblestone then goes under iron arches, and then the iron arches have ivy draping like curtains from them. The ivy then becomes roses, and the roses are the last addition before you arrive at a great iron gate with the words "Quis, Quid, Ubi, Quibus Auxiliis, Cur, Quomodo, Quando" written in iron. The gate is wide open as it always is during open hours, and the Ipswich Library stands just ahead.

"My word, it's glorious!" breathes Soleil, admiring the building that I too have admired my whole life, though I am not sure why. The Ipswich Library is like a castle, a shack, a mansion, and a garden all in one—with lots of books.

The massive stone building has a thatched roof of all things and many chimneys, turrets—yes, turrets—and statues of kings, queens, winged children, and winged animals. The statues do not seem to match the overall look of the building, but because everything about it is so unusual, they don't seem out of place. Now that I am familiar with Emily, I know what these creatures are about. I had no clue before.

As we approach the building, I look at the library's windows. There are many windows of all sizes and shapes, and a flowerpot is in every one. As a kid, I liked to scare myself by imagining a ghost suddenly appearing in one of them. I still do that.

We make our way to the stone steps that lead to the front doors—two golden doors with half-moon windows on each one and white pig's snout doorknockers. Atticus opens one and holds it for the rest of us to go in before himself. The library's front door opens to a grand, open room. Two staircases wrap up each side to more smaller rooms. A secretary's desk is directly in front of us, where a small yet tall woman sits smiling at us. Dangling chains hang from her pointed glasses, and her grin seems to reach each point. She is dressed in a smart suit with a line of black buttons down her shirt with a ruffled collar.

"Well, hello. Welcome to Little Ipswich Library. Good to see you again, Master Wes. Long time no see, Miss Maggie. Who do we have here?" She smiles at Atticus, Calysta, and Soleil—but mostly Soleil.

"Hi, Miss Squaffletree," pipes Wes. "Do we have a story for you!"

Chapter 3
Miss Squaffletree is Safe

Miss Squaffletree looks amused at Wes. "My, how the tables have turned, Master Wes. It is usually I who has the story for *you*."

Soleil steps forward extending her hand to Miss Squaffletree. "I apologize, Miss Squatty, but we will have to tell you the story another time. We are in such a hurry. Could you, by chance, point me in the direction of *Alchemy and Elixirs* by Kenrick Grimm?"

Miss Squaffletree's head cocks to one side. "I'm not sure we have that particular selection in stock. It doesn't sound familiar— or modern, for that matter... *you remind me of someone.*" Her eyes squint at Soleil but not in a bad way.

Taken a little aback at being recognized, Soleil looks at all of us kids.

"It's alright," I say. "She's safe. We've known Miss Squaffletree since before we were in school. She's very kind."

Miss Squaffletree's soft but curious eyes meet mine, and I can tell we both remember all the times she sat with Wes and me talking about all the fantastic things we were reading in the books we picked. Along with the stories themselves, she knew all about the authors and the backstories of the stories. She would explain things we didn't quite yet understand and even take us to her "special shelf" hidden in the Reference Section that she only showed to "true book lovers." She has been wonderful to us and is the main reason Wes and I have read as much as we have. "We can trust her."

Miss Squaffletree's eyes are now not only soft and curious but glistening. Wes goes to her and reaches up to put a hand on her shoulder. "Miss Squaffletree, meet Queen Soleil Everly, queen of Whitescale House and mistress of math and sciences."

The librarian gawks at Soleil. A choking sound comes from her, and she loses her footing a bit. Trying to compose herself, she blurts, "I knew it! But—but it's impossible! You—the ancestors—you're all—"

All of us are grinning at Miss Squaffletree's reaction to the "resurrected dead."

"That's the long story we don't have time to tell, madame. I do apologize. Now if you could help me possibly find a book similar—"

"No, no, that's not why I brought you here," Wes interrupts. "Come with me."

Everyone, even Miss Squaffletree still mouth agape, follows Wes up the stairs and into a long corridor. We pass several doors with things like "Renaissance," and "Cuisine," and "A Wee Bit Scary" on them. At one point, we pass a sign that reads, "Turn Back! Nothing to See Here!" but Wes keeps going until we finally come to a door that says, "Oh, Alright, If You Must," and enter the computer lab.

Soleil gawks awkwardly at the room of computers and, without warning, puts her nose to one of the screens, then pecks a few keys with her finger. When the screen changes, she gasps. "Sorcery!"

"Probably," says Atticus.

"It's a computer, Queen Soleil," says Wes. "I'm going to help you find what you need on the internet."

"A net?" She looks around the room. "Where is the net? In that flat box?"

"No, not that kind of net. I'll break it all down for you later, but for now, tell me what you need, and I'll look for it."

Soleil deflates. "Alright, but please do, er, break it down for me later. I must know what this magic is all about," she says, waving her fingers at the computer. Unable to help herself, she examines the back of the monitor. "How in the world do those pictures get in there? Certainly otherworldly."

"Try to focus, Queen Soleil," pleads Wes.

"Oh, I'm so sorry, my dear boy. Yes, let's get to work." She sits unsteadily in the swiveling chair beside him, never taking her eyes away from the screen.

"Do we need to stay?" I ask. "I want to look around a bit."

There is nothing worse than waiting around for Wes to find something online. The problem is that he always finds a bunch of other things too, keeping him on for hours.

"No, Maggie, we'll come down when we're done. Maybe fill Miss S. in," Wes says while bringing up the search engine.

Miss Squaffletree clasps her hands together in glee. "That sounds like a splendid idea!"

Soleil rattles off a list of foreign items to Wes, including marine snails and tourmaline. We all turn to leave as Wes frantically runs a search for the items. Then, just as we begin to descend the stairs, we hear Soleil pipe, "It's useless!"

"It isn't. These are very obscure things, Your Majesty," replies Wes, still typing away. "Just wait. I'm not finished."

"Alchemy has long been proven false, Soleil," I call to them.

"Ah, I can see how it has," Soleil calls back thoughtfully. "But there is always something true in every myth, Princess."

"Is there a place here where we can talk privately, Miss Squaffletree?"

"Certainly." Miss Squaffletree makes her way past us and then leads us back down the stairs and to a room in the back. We've arrived at a door with the number eighteen on it. Miss Squaffletree removes a set of keys from her pocket and unlocks the door. Inside is a room with only bookshelves for walls. There is a desk with a lamp and a nameplate reading Elexess Squaffletree. Each corner of this room has different cozy setups for one to sit and read. One is a squashy, floral armchair with a candle on the table beside it. One is a rocker with a single Edison light hanging from the ceiling. One is a luxurious chaise lounge with a soft light positioned over the reader's shoulder, and the last and most spectacular, in my opinion, is a single bed with a kettle on the nightstand and a window picture of a rainy day.

"Is this your office? It's amazing!" I exclaim.

"Yes, it is, my dear. I'm a librarian. We are all at least a little bit eccentric. But if you ask me, it's just practical. You never know what kind of reading mood will strike. Take a seat anywhere you fancy."

Atticus takes the chaise lounge, Calysta the armchair, leaving the bed for me. I plop down, my legs hanging off the side. Miss Squaffletree sits behind her desk looking expectant, so the three of us try to fill her in as quickly as we can everything that has occurred.

She listens silently, awe-struck with little gasps here and there. When we've told her as much as there is time for today, she is speechless, a common reaction of those hearing the story for the first time.

"I have absolutely no words. Except, of course, for these I'm saying right now."

"Please don't tell anyone just yet, Miss S. Let us get sorted out first," I tell her.

"You have my word, but please allow me and the library to help however we can. There is no limit to the power of words."

"Thank you. I'm sure we'll need you," I reply.

Miss Squaffletree leans back in her chair crossing her arms.

"This may sound cheeky, but I knew there was something off about Emily. I can't explain it, but I could sense it. Everything was, on the surface, perfect—yet dark somehow. When I was young my parents asked me if I wanted to attend Emily Academy. I declined. To me, there is nothing more magical than this library my family began so long ago. I thought that then and still now to this day. I have never regretted my decision."

"I would say you made the right one, Miss Squaffletree," says Calysta.

"Agreed. But I bet Soleil and Wes are close to finding what they are looking for. We should check," Atticus reminds us.

"Right. Let's go," I say, standing up first. We all exit room eighteen, and just as Atticus thought, Wes and Soleil are descending the stairs.

Wes looks uneasy. "Soleil says she's gotta go find what she needs for alchemy."

Soleil nods looking determined.

"What? Where? How long will that take?" I ask.

"Not to worry, Princess. I shall take Zelda, and we should return from Brazil and Mozambique in no time."

"Brazil and Mozambique!" We all say in unison.

Wes looks even more uneasy, and now Soleil does too. "And Connecticut," she adds.

"Connecticut!" We all exclaim in unison again.

"I must go. I must retrieve the ingredients to stop the Einsreich, and Brazil, Mozambique, and Connecticut are where they are. Come. We must get going. I need to get Zelda, and you know the others will put up a fuss."

Speechless, we follow Soleil zombie-like to the library's main entrance. Miss Squaffletree bids us farewell. "I will be keeping an eye toward the castle from now on," she tells us, opening one of the golden doors. "Thank you for informing me. You now have one more in your fight."

"Thanks, Miss S.," Wes replies, hugging Miss Squaffletree around her waist.

"How will you know what's going on there?" I ask her.

Behind her pointed glasses, the librarian winks. "I told you. There is power in words, Maggie. More than anyone could imagine. Libraries are the hub of the world."

A little annoyed at her secret-keeping, I smile and shrug.

"Be safe," Miss Squaffletree warns as we pass her out the doors. "Oh, wait!" she exclaims suddenly and runs back into the library. She emerges again with a small red basket. "For you all!" She hands the basket to Calysta.

"Lucky nests?" Calysta says. "At the library?"

"Why, of course, Miss Calysta. The library had them first. Everything, and I do mean everything, begins with words."

Chapter 4
Remember, Maggie

Wearily, we start back toward the Boggletrice Company headquarters, walking slowly to avoid rushing upon an Einsreich. Calysta passes the basket of lucky nests to each of us. Why can I not seem to get away from these things? But everyone happily takes one, and not wanting to draw attention, I take one too.

Soleil smiles as she opens hers. "You know, we don't have lucky nests in Brumbletide."

"Really?" says Atticus already munching. "Seems like these of all things would be there. There is something magical about them. They always seem to know what's going to happen."

"Ah, indeed, they do, Prince Atticus. But no harm befalls us in Brumbletide. Pippin only sends lucky nests where they are needed. But we do, in fact, have very extraordinary and magical desserts—ones you could never imagine. My favorite being one that burns up before you only to have a divinity phoenix rise from the rubble."

"Wow! Blimey, can you imagine nothing ever going

wrong?" Atticus asks the rest of us. "What does everyone do all day?" He reads his lucky nest aloud. "O, Champion, prepare for a bloody endeavor." He chokes a little.

"Are you alright, Prince Atticus?" Soleil whacks him on the back. The lucky nest seems to dislodge, and he is okay. Seeing he isn't choking, Soleil continues her talk of Brumbletide. "There is a ton to do in a land with no wrong. Not only do you have more than enough time to be with your loved ones, but there is *work* to be done. Hard work cultivating *life*. You all, as well as we who help you deal with your suffering, are used to having so much wrong that you can't fathom life being any other way. But there was both Life and Work before Darkness, and Life and Work will continue on after Darkness."

"Gosh, it's so hard to comprehend," says Calysta, smoothing out her little scroll from her lucky nest which she's already eaten. "Once blind, twice a victor. Once stone, thrice predictor." She glances at the rest of us but receives only shrugs. "Weird. What does yours say Maggie?"

"I haven't opened mine yet."

"Well, what are you waiting for?" Calysta asks.

I sigh and break apart the biscuit, but when Calysta asks Wes about his, I shove everything into my pocket.

Wes reads his lucky nest, scratching his head. "It's strange."

"No surprise there," I say.

"A safe place you must find. Cover the tracks left behind."

"Hmm," Atticus puts his fingers to his chin. "Lucky nests always have a way of creeping me out. Safe place? That insinuates you'd be in a dangerous place first, right?"

"Hope not." But Wes's eyes widen. "But maybe this is my chance to be like Morto and Ornius," he says dreamily.

Soleil looks curiously at Calysta and me. "Depths of the Deminsions. It's a game," I tell her.

Soleil brightens. "I love games! Prince Wesley, promise you will teach me this Depths of the Dimensions."

My brother suddenly becomes teary, and his voice cracks. "Oh, I'd be honored, Queen Soleil."

"Wonderful," Soleil beams.

"What does yours say, Queen Soleil?" asks Calysta.

"I almost forgot. Let's see." She examines her scroll with furrowed brows. "Find the Golden Blood Warmouth." She stares at the words as if trying to decipher a puzzle.

"What in the world is that?" asks Calysta.

Soleil speaks more to herself than any of us. "I have heard of such a thing through the years. But it is impossible to retrieve. It's only legend."

"What kind of warmouth is it?" I ask.

"No one knows. But the legend goes that when Michelle killed Pippin in the Battle of Crescent and Fall, that one warmouth had died and was lying dead on the field."

"How awful!" pipes Calysta.

"Oh, Calysta, it was. I cannot thoroughly describe to you how awful that battle really was. But the story goes that when Pippin's blood poured from his heart the way it did—that really did happen—that one warmouth was covered in it. And after everyone had gone, days later, they came back to life and are still flying the earth somewhere."

"That's amazing!" cries Calysta.

But I see a glaring problem with Soleil's story. "We have no way of knowing if it's true. And even according to the legend, no one would have seen it, would they? I mean, you just said everyone had gone when it happened."

"But Maggie, why would the lucky nest say to find it then?" asks Wes.

"I'm just saying we've reached a bunch of dead ends already and shouldn't go down trails that might lead to nowhere."

None of my friends respond, but there is a negative air now that I have caused. "But hey, maybe!" I add, hoping to reverse the damage.

We've approached the bridge, and to our relief, there are no Einsreich. The tension visibly releases as we walk into Downtown Ipswich—that is, except for Calysta. "Everything looks alright, but I have a terrible feeling that something bad is about to happen."

My attempt at reversal has not worked.

The town is its usual bustle at this time of day. Everyone is busy with their own business but still stops to glance at the bunch of crown-wearers. We pass the barber and the bakery, but when we pass Mr. Peabody's practice, Atticus ducks behind the rest of us in case his dad happens to be looking out his window. The coast is clear, but not for long. As we approach the first alleyway, all of the Einsreich that had been dispersed around the town have now congregated. Slumped, pale princes and princesses lumber out of the alley with their heads down but quickly approaching us.

"Run!" shouts Atticus, and we all scatter. I didn't see where the others went; I just hope they are finding safety. I fly as fast as I can to the oak tree in the center of town. Rounding the massive trunk, I crouch down to peek back at the alley to see if I can see any of the others. A large academy student lumbers after Wes who is speeding away toward Lazy Jug. *Don't show them where the headquarters are, Wes.* He's smarter than that.

A strong grip yanks my arm, and I am caught in a tight embrace with a hand over my mouth. "Time for school, Maggie." It's the cool and condescending voice of Tritch Anguis.

Hidden behind the hulking oak of Downtown Ipswich, a coat is thrown over me, and I am dragged to a white limousine, where Tritch shoves me inside. King Klauschwitz is already in the car with two Einsreich princes. I feel the edge of Tritch's hand on my lip and bite with everything I have.

"Ahhhh! You filthy girl!" he shouts but doesn't take his hand away. He presses hard on my face as I struggle to get away.

"Sephtis, Orpheus, fetch!" commands Klauschitz.

The two zombie princes easily grab hold of me, and I don't know if it is Sephtis or Orpheus, but one squeezes me until all goes dark.

I blink open my eyes in a place that has become very familiar to me. The curtain of my canopy bed is open. The torchless flames are lit on the chandelier. I am unaware what time it is, but it is before curfew. Thorn sits at her desk working away at something—definitely not homework. There are no warmouths anywhere. I have been changed into a white gown, the palace garments. My street clothes are folded on a chair by my wardrobe.

I am too overwhelmed to try to get away or even be outraged. I stay still, hoping that I will eventually wake up and this will have been one long and terrible dream.

Thorn glances up from her work and finally notices my open eyes. She puts down her quill and comes over, crossing her arms and leaning against her bedpost. She wears a gorgeous silver gown with lots of frilly texture. Heads of Castle do not have to wear white like everyone else. I remember Lenore saying she hated wearing white like us "commonwealth."

"Maggie, you've got to stop trying to fight. You have no chance of winning. Have you seen how many Einsreich there are? And they're only going to keep coming. You're going to get yourself killed."

"Pretty sure that's what you all plan to do to me anyway. Seems like *you* could do something about all of this if you wanted to, being in charge in all," I say dully.

She doesn't reply. She and I both know Thorn isn't actually in charge of anything.

"Maggie, there's nothing I can do. My dad and Klauschwitz are going to keep you alive, but only so no one asks questions."

"How nice," I mutter. "People are asking about me?"

"They're going to make you tell them where the others are, Maggie."

"What others?" I ask, playing dumb.

Thorn rolls her eyes. "Stop it. This is serious. Dad and Klauschwitz saw Soleil with you."

So she wasn't caught then.

"I have no idea what you're talking about. Where are my friends? Where's Wes?"

"That's what we need you to tell us."

They weren't caught either! I say nothing, careful not to give away a single detail.

Thorn looks at my face, searching. "You're going to have to tell. I'm telling you, they will make you tell. You have no idea what they'll do to you to get information."

"Oh? Something like what they do to Snickerlings, possibly? Slaughter them to cut out their tongues and wings?"

I find myself exceedingly thankful that somehow we have managed to keep Thorn from knowing about the Boggletrice Company headquarters. She's even been to Brumbletide but never to the headquarters.

"What time is it? What day?"

"It's mid-morning on Tuesday. We're between periods—almost time for High Noon Fare. You have to come. My father needs you to act as normal as possible."

"Well then, I will act as abnormal as possible for his sake."

Thorn huffs. "You don't want to do that."

"I don't want to do any of this!"

"Calm down," Thorn says quietly. "I've got to go to class. A Snickerling will bring your schedule soon. You're being watched constantly, even in here. Keep that in mind when you're changing."

I say nothing. Thorn gets her satchel and heads to class. I get up out of bed, unsure of what to do. Of course Pippin hasn't visited me in real life or my dreams, and he's nowhere to be found.

I open my wardrobe to see what's in it. My Little Ipswich duffle is gone. The only thing I have here is the clothes I wore from home when I was captured. I pick them up. I can smell Mrs. Cloudt's cooking, and my heart breaks again, but differently this time. Everything has gone so wrong so many times now, and sometimes, I can't remember what we're fighting for. I wad up my jacket but feel something inside. Checking the pockets, I find the lucky nest I didn't want to read. The paper is the only thing not crushed into dust. Reluctantly, I take the tiny parchment and read it.

Only two words: *Remember, Maggie.*

Brynn Miller, age 12

Brynn Miller, age 12

Chapter 5
Rexes and Reginas

At High Noon Fare, you'd never guess where I am sitting—at a table on the Throne Room floor with none other than Emily's Head of Academy, King Klauschwitz, Tritch Anguis, and Thorn. Wow, what an honor.

Einsreich are everywhere. At least one behemoth royal is on each balcony, and they encircle the floor, standing like ominous statues. Their heads and arms hang forward like willows in a cemetery.

One extremely blatant change is that the Snickerlings no longer fly around the Throne Room or anywhere for that matter. I know the Einsreich render them powerless because Jericho could not do anything magical when they captured us and took us to the dungeon. I wonder what lie has been told to the students about why the Sickerlings aren't flying anymore. Now that the Snickerlings can't fly, white carpets have been enchanted somehow to fly on their own, and whatever kind of dark magic has been used doesn't work very well. Our High Noon Fare feast was brought to us on wobbly carpets that drop food and drink here and there and everywhere. Eden Kung received a wash of Bubblegin right on top of his head, and Missy Orr screamed when a large plate of sandwiches landed in her lap.

"How did you make the carpets fly on their own?" I ask Tritch.

"I don't remember permitting you to speak, but if you must know, the Einsreich provide magic of their very own," Tritch says coolly, sipping soup from a spoon. He winces at the taste. "A little more perfecting of these fine specimens, and Emily will have no need for Snickerlings anymore."

I stare in horror. What will happen to them then? A glimmer of hope says they'll return to Brumbletide, but recent history seems to tell a more accurate story: once the Snickerlings are no longer needed as servants, there will be a massive slaughtering for their magic. I squeeze my eyes shut and shudder.

"Buck up, Maggie. You won't have to worry long. Eat." Tritch says without looking away from his soup.

I pick at my pumpkin dumpling, too repulsed to think about eating. The pumpkin dumpling is disgusting, and I realize the entire feast is burned and ugly—more Einsreich magic. The Snickerlings aren't able to create the delicious feasts they could before.

A few trumpets sound from some Snickerlings standing on a high balcony. King Klauschwitz leaves our table and goes to the middle of the room by a Snickerling boy holding many medals. The chatty students quiet down. Klauschwitz clears his throat, and it occurs to me that I've never heard him speak. His voice is much higher than I thought it would be yet drawling, but the thing that stands out most has nothing to do with his actual voice. We are all startled, and some even scream when his voice is not amplified by the Snickerlings as usual but by the Einsreich, who distort his voice in a sinister jerking growl that makes your skin crawl. Since the Snickerlings cannot amplify voices anymore, Klauschwitz's voice comes from the Einsreich, and as it does, it is eerie, broken, and distorted. "R-royals of Eh-emily Academy. The time has co-oooome to announce this year's Rexes and Reginas and much too late late late because of the myriaaa-aaad of unplanned changes-changes-changes Emily has experienced. Rexes and Reginaaaa-aaas are royals who will-will be leaders of their hooo-oo-ooouses this year because they have displayed both a-a-academic and social exceeeeellence at the a-a-academy. Rexes and Reginaaaaas at my former academy, Infernum, have gone on to be extra-extra-extraaaaa-ooooordinary forces in the world. I have no doubt the same will be said for Eh-Eh-Emily's."

Ha! Extraordinarily evil forces, I think to myself.

"Queen Mothers, please riiiiiiise to ah-ah-announce your choices."

The seven Queen Mothers at their table on the other end of the Throne Room rise, looking quite uneasy, and line up behind Klauschwitz. It may be just me, but they all appear very tired.

"Queeeeeen Motherrrrrs, please be sh-sh-short since we are still perf-perf-perfecting our new sound-sound-sound system."

Queen Mother Felberta comes forth first. Even though she hasn't spoken, I can tell she is back to her usual pleasant self. Not long ago, she was possessed by Michelle when given a ruby crown by Thorn that the spirit of Michelle had inhabited. "Royals of Eh-Emilyyyyy, oh-oh dear, I am pleeeeeaaased to ah-annooooouunce—oh heaven's sake. Whitescales, your Rex is Copernicus Fish. Your-your Regina is Sophie Germain," she says as fast as she can, shaking her head in frustration with the Einsreich. Even so, she leads the room in an applause for Copernicus and Sophie, who are not flown to the floor by Snickerlings, but their medals are flown to them by an unsteady and unmanned carpet that dumps them into their balconies. Copernicus and Sophie receive their medals, hang them around their necks, and wave to their peers.

Toadie is next to announce the Firebreathers. "Firebreatherrrrrs, your Reeeex is-is-is star student, Damien Barbas."

And your Regina is Thorn Anguis. No surprise.

"Your Regina is-is-is not my choice, but that oooooof of the neeeeew Head of of of A-A-Academy, Kiiiing Klauschwitz." Her ugly, warty face scowls as if her next words leave a bad taste in her mouth. "Your Regina is Maggie Prewitt."

What?

The Snickerling places one medal on the carpet that is flown, though dropped once, to Damien Barbas.

"Get up! Yoooouuuu have leeeeegs!" shouts Toadi through the Einsreich.

I jump up and hurry to the Snickerling who places the dragon medal around my neck. I curtsy and eye Tritch and Thorn on the way back to the table. Tritch's face is straight, and he doesn't clap. Thorn picks at her feast.

"What's this about?" I ask, sitting back down.

"You have not been permitted to speak," says Tritch without looking away from the Queen Mothers and Klauschwitz.

Queen Mother Berthilda of Champion House is next. She gets straight to the point. "Champion Rex is Jordan McShane. Regina is Graciee-eeee Heart." She applauds heartily as the Champion medals are flown to their owners.

Queen Mother Hertha announces Everest Rhoades and Berkley Hawthorne as Bravetail's Rex and Regina; Queen Mother Erline announces Wolfgang Oliver and Giada Galetti as Fleetwing's.

Queen Mother Carrington has the least amount of swagger I've ever seen her with but is still cool and collected despite the strange situation. She refuses to speak through the Einsreich and, smirking, only points to Tristan Chambers and Madonna Winters as the Fairfang Rex and Regina.

Queen Mother Stiorri does speak through the Einsreich. She huffs, saying, "B-b-bear with me, friiiiieeends." And her voice crookedly calls on Jeremiah Potter and Debbie Judge, who receive their medals happily.

Klauschwitz gives a quick salutation, and everyone returns to their feast. When he sits at the table, still no one mentions that I am the Firebreather Regina.

"What class do you have next, Maggie?" Thorn asks.

"Michelle Academics."

"Brilliant," says Tritch brightly. "Queen Mother Toadi is the most excellent of our staff by far. Enjoy."

I frown.

The trumpets sound, and we are all wonkily carried by Einsreich-powered carpets to our classes. I grip the edge of the carpet tightly for dear life, screaming as the carpet ascends Michelle Tower at an almost vertical incline. The conical roof opens, and I am dropped stories down into the tower. I plunge to my death, only narrowly escaping it by landing on a chaise lounge that cracks on impact.

Queen Mother Toadi watches me with a scowl. "If you had parents, they would be getting a bill for that," she snips.

I want to scream. I want to yell. I want to punch the squatty toad woman in her fat, warty face—and I still might. But if there is one thing I have learned in this crazy journey so far, it is that acting impulsively rarely works out well.

There is, of course, no Atticus or Calysta in class with me today. I did not see Wes in the halls because he isn't here. Sadness washes out the anger. I sit next to Cecilia Hernandez, who looks me up and down as if she were seeing a ghost. "Maggie, you've got to tell us what's going on around here. We're all creeped out but afraid to say anything. A bunch of us thought they must have expelled you since we didn't see you anymore. And that stuff you were saying at the Em Games, is it true? At first, it all seems ridiculous but now I'm not so sure." She eyes my Regina medal.

"Silence!" yells Toadi. "You should have chatted at High Noon Fare. Now is the time for execution."

Cecilia and I each take one of the books stacked on the coffee tables.

"Begin with *A Tale of a King*, King Michelle's biography. An essay on chapters one through nine is due next class. No talking."

We all begin reading. I open *A Tale of a King*. Surprisingly, the front cover has a picture of a crown between two great white antlers. How did *that* make it into the book? I flip to the forward written by Rufus Foxenbrand, BCE 57.

This is the account of how the king of all kings, Pippin the great White Stag, created Ipswich and the land that will be known as Brumbletide, a Promised Land foretold for centuries. This book is good and true and not to be added to or taken away from. Anyone who changes so much as a dash will never be welcome in the great kingdom of Brumbletide and will receive the due penalty for their sin.

I blink several times to see if I am really reading what I am reading. What in the world?

Chapter 1: Singing into Existence

When the earth was formless and void, there was Pippin. At that time, he was not the Stag you know him as now, but the Stag was with him and in him and was him. Long ago, before any history was written, Pippin sang into existence light in the void and shortly after sang into existence the first Snickerlings, warmouths, and Horsemen. They lived together in the void and Pippin provided abundantly for his creatures. He loved every one.

What the? I flip through the book.

Chapter 5: The Creation of Ipswich...

Chapter 7: The Fall of the Dragon...

This book is all about Pippin! I look around the tower. Every royal is engrossed in *A Tale of a King,* reading with furrowed brows. I glance over at Cecilia Hernandez's copy. Chapter one says the same thing as mine! How? Why on earth would they allow us to read this?

A Snickerling girl is carried by an Einsreich-powered carpet into the tower and dumped inside. She lands hard on a Fleetwing boy who yelps. "Oh, I am most sorry, Prince Matthew,' she pleads before scurrying to Toadi. She curtsies and hands the Queen Mother a stack of bound parchment. "The files you requested, Queen Mother Toadi."

"Leave them on the desk," Toadi replies rudely with her large nostrils in the air.

I watch with sadness as the Snickerling sets the stack on Toadi's desk and nervously boards the erratic carpet again that flies her up and out of the tower at a vertical incline.

Watching the Snickerling's ghastly exit, it's like a lightbulb blows up in my brain. The Einsreich have their own magic that Tritch and Klauschwitz are utilizing now. The Snickerlings are rendered useless—but it is the Snickerling magic that has kept this castle going all these years. It is the Snickerling magic that has transformed the library books into lies about Michelle! Tritch and Klauschwitz have accidentally brought back the truth to the people! What will they do when they realize?

Chapter 6
Heated Thoughts

The trumpets blast at the end of Michelle Academics, and Toadi announces that all students and staff have been called to a meeting in the Throne Room.

Cecilia Hernandez and I are on an erratic carpet together with two other students, and by the time we make it to the Throne Room, we are battered and bruised but thankful to be alive. The carpet dumps the others into a high balcony but somehow keeps me on, and I am flown back to my "privileged" space at Tritch's table. King Klauschwitz is standing behind a podium on a dais. He must be the one giving the announcement. When all the academy royals are panting and gasping in a balcony from their death-defying carpet rides, King Klauschwitz begins his address. His voice jolts and snags. "Fine royals of Eh-Emily, lend me your majestic ee-ears. It has been brought to my ah-ah-attention that many of you are unnerved by theeeeeee recent changes to Emily. I want to take this time to-to-to put you at eeee-ease."

No one is at ease. Not one.

"Never would we dream of haaaaarming you-you. We hold our a-a-academy students in only the hi-highest regaaaaard, and weeeeeee take pride in our graduates being be-be-beacons of liiiiiight in the world that reflect the gaaaaaaze of the public back to uuuu-uuuus. Why would weeeeeee then do anything anything anything other than treeeeeaaat you well and giiiiiive you the best possible groooo-ooooming here? Truuu-uuue, there have been many changes happening in recent weeks, and while while while they may seeeeeeem drastic and, as some may thiiiii-iiiink, for the wooooorse, I assure you it only seeeeems so because it is unfamiliar. You seeeeeeeeee, while previous administrations have excelled iiiiiiiin grooming you all into your roooo-oooo-yal des-des-destiny, it has failed in one iiiiiiimportant area—di-di-di-diiiiiiiversity. You are uncomfortable with Emily's new students because they are diiiiiiiifferent from yourselves. These next words will sting sting sting a bit, but my yooooooung princesssss and princessesssss, growth often includes pain pain pain pain. This is well and gooooood. You are uneasy toward the Infernum transfers be-be-because of your prejudiiiiiiiices. As the beacons of light thaaaat you are to beeeeeeee, let me be clear, you musssssssst overcome your prejudiiiiiiiiices and accept those unlike yourselvesssssss."

The room is rigid and silent. I roll my eyes. What a load of—

"I challeeee-eeeeenge you all to not dweeeeeell on this. Ov-ov-overthinking will only strengthen your prejudiiiiiiiiiices. Act. You mu-mu-must be swiiiiiift to act. This is all iiiiiiiin the naaaaaaaame of looooooooooove love-love-love looooooove-love-looooooove-looooooove." The Einsreich have hit a major snag. Klauschwitz pauses to give them time to recalibrate.

"Thaaaaa-aaaaaat." He pauses again. "That is all we have time for to-to-today. You must get back to claaaaassssssss, your ma-ma-majesties. But remeeeeeeember, all in the name of lo-lo-lo-lo-loooooooove."

The students, only doing what they have been trained to do at Emily Academy, try to recite the awry benediction with Klauschwitz's distorted Einsreich-amplified voice as they board the carpets from hell. Thorn and I both have Non-Common Sense, so we ride together, and I finally see Thorn on the verge of freaking out as the carpet almost drops us into the Lux twice. Others are not so lucky. Missy Orr and Graisse Anguis's carpet throws them off, and they both splash into the sea.

Every royal in Non-Common Sense is solemn. Queen Mother Stiorri informs us that we will be doing exercises that do not include magic of any kind since there seems to be a short circuit going on.

"Has this ever happened before, Queen Mother?" asks Cecilia Hernandez.

"Never, Princess Cecilia. It is very peculiar, and I must admit unnerving."

Queen Mother Stiorri has us sit at our ancient desks with our hands clasped in front of us. "Clasping your hands seems insignificant, but it is crucial for the effectiveness of this exercise."

The class is now still and quiet at our desks, positioned as requested.

"Now, class, today we will try to *feel* the emotions connected to certain events in your life. We are going to remember what happened and really pick apart your emotions from the event as to how they affected you positively and negatively. Close your eyes."

I close my eyes.

Queen Mother Stiorri instructs us in a soft voice. "We will begin with the first thing that had any significant impact on you, good or bad. Get the memory in your mind."

I think back to the first thing I really loved in life, Nan's Pancakes with Dad.

"Get the image of the scene in your mind's eye and really explore it. Every detail, every nook, every cranny. Use your five senses."

I hear the sizzle of bacon and smell its saltiness amid coffee and syrup. Divine. I liked to eat the pancake and bacon together in salty-sweet goodness. I see the starry night outside the diner's windows. I see Dad smiling at me, coffee mug in hand. My heart flutters and my eyes burn with tears.

But I feel something else too. Energy is welling up in my crown. The obsidian! My memories—oh no. Memories fuel the power of the obsidian stone in my crown!

I squeeze my eyes shut and try to extinguish the memory of Dad and Nan's, but the energy is still there and continues to well up. The pressure builds. I'm going to have to do something, or my head is going to explode. But if I put my fingers to my crown, the power will release and blast something. *What do I do? What do I do?*

I open one eye. Everyone's eyes are closed. Queen Mother Stiorri paces the room, and her back is to me at the moment. It's now or never. I aim my crown at the floor in front of my desk and silently put two fingers to my crown. Red light flashes down, pushing the straps of Cecilia Hernandez's satchel a little. Thank heavens, it was a happy memory!

The light is dimming when Queen Mother Stiorri turns around. She looks at the dim red light. She looks at me. She looks at my crown. Her wide eyes meet mine.

"I-I need to go to the loo, Queen Mother."

Mouth hanging, Queen Mother Stiorri motions for me to go. "Quickly, Princess."

I swiftly vacate Eve Tower, running down the winding staircase that ends at Ironsnout Hall. I decide to use the loo nearest the Remembering Hall to see what the castle is like there now that the Einsreich have taken over. It is lined with Einsreich, and no Snickerlings are soaring anywhere. A frog hops from beneath a lumbering Einsreich prince. Repulsed by both the frog and the prince, I continue on to the loo, but I don't make it five steps before I stop again, this time at the familiar voice near the drawbridge.

"Yes, that's right. My name is Elexess Squaffletree, and this is my nephew, Ernest Finebaum. I need to speak with the admissions director, please. He has no family, and now that he is in my care, I want him to attend this academy."

Hiding behind a suit of armor that I realize is a statue of George, I watch Miss Squaffletree and Ernie. What are they doing? I'm anxious for them, but my heart leaps at the same time.

King Abner is back at his station shaking his head. "I understand, ma'am, but while it is all well and good that you desire your nephew to attend Emily Academy, enrollment doesn't open until July."

"Nonsense! He'll be too far behind by then. He cannot wait. I will not leave until I have spoken to the admissions director." Miss Squaffletree crosses her arms and stamps her foot. Ernie slumps quietly at her side.

"I'm afraid it is not only that." King Abner hesitates. "I'm afraid the magic of the castle has been having some, er, hiccups. As you can see, our renowned Snickerlings aren't flying the Remembering Hall, and it was found this morning that the castle has sunk six inches into the Lux Sea."

At this, Miss Squaffletree hesitates as well. "I see." But she lifts her chin, hand on Ernie's shoulder. "Still, Ernest will attend Emily Academy, and he will attend today. I'm sure all will be fine soon. Get me the admissions director. Let *him* tell me Ernest can't enroll."

It is so strange listening to Miss Squaffletree speak so sternly. It's totally unlike her.

King Abner gives a defeated sigh and reluctantly rings his pearly handbell. An Einsreich prince lumbers over.

"Take them to King Klauschwitz," he tells the thing. The Einsreich stiffly turns and walks away. King Abner waves Miss Squaffletree and Ernie on, and they hurry after the Einsreich.

"Thank you, sir!" Miss Squaffletree calls behind her.

I hide behind the metal George even more as I watch them walk to the stairs. Just when I think no one noticed me, Miss Squaffletree quickly glances in my direction and winks. I blush and can hardly keep from giggling. Oh my, I hope they stay safe whatever they are up to. Realizing I need to get back to class, I run into the bathroom, remove the obsidian from my crown, and put it into my girdle—yes, my girdle. *Ugh.*

When I return to Non-Common Sense, Queen Mother Stiorri is already on the third exercise. She places her fingers to her lips when she sees me and comes over, whispering, "If you jump back in now, it will disrupt the class, and you won't be able to get into it either. Please stay after class so I can catch you up to speed."

I nod and go to my desk, where I watch everyone else relive their life's most traumatic moments behind their eyelids. Some faces, like Missy Orr's, are stark white, while others, like Eden Kung's, have the translucent stains of tears. To no surprise, Thorn looks exactly the same as always.

Chapter 7
Mind's Eye

The royals in Non-Common Sense gather their things to leave.

"Hey! What happened to my bag?" Cecilia calls, revealing her satchel's severed strap.

Oops. How did that happen? It was a happy memory!

Cecilia looks at me since I was sitting behind her. I must have seen *something*. I shrug.

"Take it to The Resplendent, Princess. They'll give you a new one." Queen Mother Stiorri tells Cecilia.

I stay seated at my desk as everyone exits the tower. Thorn is the last one out but hangs at the door. "Come on, Maggie."

Queen Mother Stiorri answers. "Princess Maggie missed some of the class, so she is staying to catch up."

Thorn's eyes shift between Queen Mother Stiorri and me suspiciously. "Well, don't be too late getting in. I'm exhausted," she tells me.

"I assure you this won't take long," says Stiorri.

Thorn hangs in the threshold a second more. I can tell she wants to say that her father will wonder why I'm staying in Non-Common Sense, but she turns on her heel and heads down the stairs.

Queen Mother Stiorri brings a notebook and quill and sits at the desk beside mine, scooting it as close to me as she can. She leans in even closer; I can feel her breath on my cheek as she whispers. "Speak softly, very softly, dear. Thorn will surely tell her father that you are staying after class, and they will be spying. I saw your light. What was that? The power of Eve, Daughter of Eve?"

Taken aback and unsure of whom to trust around here, I reply under my breath, "Sort of hard to explain."

Stiorri's expectant demeanor falls a bit. "Well, we need someone's power, that's for sure. I fear we are heading for very dark days here, Princess."

Heading for? It's been dark the whole time.

She leans even closer. I can almost feel her lips as she says, "I can't help but think you are here to help us, Princess. If I can help you help us, I will do anything in my limited power to do so."

I stare at the Queen Mother. *Are you really good, Queen Mother Stiorri?* I think back to Queen Mother Felberta's questioning when she was possessed by Michelle. She seemed normal at first.

"I'm not sure what you mean, Queen Mother, but if I think of something, I'll let you know."

Stiorri deflates as if I've driven an ice pick into the float she was going to use at the pool. She sighs. "Thank you. Let's get started, shall we?" She pats my arm and stands up, shifting into teacher mode again. "Close your eyes, Princess. Let's go back to the most profound event that has happened to you in your life thus far. Not tragedy—profound event. Something that has possibly changed you forever."

Well, the tragedy in my life *did* change me forever. I don't have my dad anymore! But I don't want to think about that right now anyway. Profound event? Oh yes, I know exactly the one.

"Get the scene in your mind," Queen Mother Stiorri instructs.

I am on the floor in the Throne Room as near to death as I have ever been. Pain surges through me like volts of electricity. Michelle is laughing. He has won. All is lost.

"Explore every detail of the vision. Use your five senses," Queen Mother Stiorri says softly.

I smell my flesh burned by Michelle's lightning. I feel the cold, hard marble of the Throne Room floor against my searing wounds. My head throbs. I taste blood from my nose and smell it too. I hear many sounds at once: Michelle's twisted laugh, his voice taunting me. He shouts, "Stupid swine!" at Magnus before swatting him with his fiery hands. The pig smacks the wall, squealing, and then he is quiet.

But then there is the earthquake. Only a small earthquake at first, but the distant rumbling comes swiftly closer. The rolling thunder grows louder and louder, and the marble beneath me vibrates. The earthquake drowns out all other noise. The roaring roll that I am certain is an earthquake shakes the castle. Goblets and chandeliers are clinking, and some even shatter.

"Do you have the vision, Princess Maggie? Can you see it? Can you feel it?"

"Oh, yes," I reply.

It is Pippin that comes into view now. But he was different then. He had taken the form of a majestic lion and swiftly and easily killed Michelle. There he is. I see him in my mind so clearly and vividly that my skin prickles.

"Pippin," I breathe.

"Pippin?" Queen Mother Stiorri's voice is like an anvil. "Did you say Pippin?"

I open my eyes, and the vision is gone, interrupted by Queen Mother Stiorri.

"Oh dear, I've ruined it. I am sorry, Princess Maggie. I don't know what got into me, but do you have a memory of the great White Stag?"

I look into Stiorri's doe-brown eyes. She reminds me of Eve in a way even though Eve's eyes are blue. But I mustn't be foolish. I cannot trust anyone here until I know for sure they are on Pippin's side.

"Have you ever seen Pippin, Queen Mother?"

Stiorri seems taken aback a little and even ashamed. "Sadly, I have not. I hope he will visit us one day soon. We need him more than ever."

Sorry, Queen Mother, I can't tell you. It's too risky. "I do too. I hope to see Pippin one day soon too."

"But your memory? What was it?"

"I guess I was just struck rather profoundly when I *learned* about Pippin the first time."

Stiorri frowns. Her float has sunken into the pool. "Oh, well, I can understand that, I guess. Let us continue. One more exercise. For your homework, you will write how these memories affected you good and bad, even to this very day."

I need to think of a different memory then.

"Alright, eyes closed. This time, we will revisit the most tragic thing that has happened to you so far. You are young. It's alright if it is something that seems silly. Everyone's worst day is their worst day."

My stomach churns, and I wince. Ugh.

"I know this is no fun. I promise good will come from this."

I am, of course, in Lazy Jug. Dad is seated with Gary and the man I would later learn is King Julian, Emily's Head of Academy. Dad thought he was just some guy at the pub.

"Get the vision good in your mind, dear, and then explore. Use all your senses."

I see Gus pouring beer. He winks at me when he sees me. The pub smells musty and liquory. I see Dad hunched at the table with cards in hand. His face is red and beaded with sweat. He hadn't been drinking very long that day; the poison was already setting in. My eyes well with tears behind their lids. I hear the raspy voice of Julian, "Uh oh, Guy's got a lil' visitor again."

I feel the starch in Dad's shirt that had wrinkled because he had slept in it the night before. I hear him yell at me for being impatient and wanting him to come eat the spaghetti I made. I feel ice in my veins all over again seeing the color drain from his face and his eyes roll back in his head. I hear my own blood-curdling scream as he falls. I hear Gus shout for a doctor. I feel and smell the blood from his nose on my skin as I do my best to breathe life into him. I am weightless with utter disbelief of the moment.

"Princess," Queen Mother Stiorri says quietly.

I realize I am crying. When I open my eyes, Stiorri is holding an embroidered handkerchief out to me. I take it and dry my tears. "I'm sorry. I've recently lost my dad. It feels both forever ago and only yesterday."

"Oh, Princess, how awful! These exercises are exceptionally healing when done well, but I must say, most royals here have not experienced such tragedy yet in their life. This acts more as a tool for the future. Oh, Princess, and here you are, away from your family when you need them most. Grief should never be navigated alone."

I say nothing.

Queen Mother Stiorri raises a brow. "You do have family? Your mother?"

I do have the Boggletrice Company and the Chosen, but we can't seem to stay together for very long.

"Your mother, darling?" Stiorri says again, searching.

I shake my head.

"Oh, Princess!" She sits back down at the desk by me and grabs my hand. "Oh, dear. Oh, dear!"

Her kind gesture releases the waterworks, and my eyes gush tears. Queen Mother Stiorri pulls me into an embrace. "That's it, darling, let it all out. Let it all out now."

I can't help but imagine Stiorri is Eve, and I dig my face into her shoulder and sob. Queen Mother Stiorri pets my hair softly with her fingers.

"Princess Maggie, I know you don't know me well, and as far as grief therapy, I'm afraid I will be of no help tonight. That is long and tedious work, but I will tell you that when I watched you in the Ironsnout event at the Em Games, I had never seen a princess demonstrate such strength and bravery. And to have never done anything like that before!"

Her encouraging words are enough to stop my sobbing. I think back to Defend the Queen when I had to, quite literally, fight the fears of all the Emily students. "Thank you, Queen Mother." My words are muffled in her gown.

"It is true, Princess—every word. I was awe-struck. I should have said something to you. I was going to! But there was a tree there I had never seen before. A gleaming, magical tree in the wood. No one seemed to notice it. It took my attention, dear. I was so intrigued. But I should have told you how proud I was of you that day."

The Silver Birch! Stiorri saw the Silver Birch! And suddenly, it's like her mention of the Silver Birch jogs my memory, and I remember Queen Mother Carrington telling me that she and Queen Mother Stiorri knew what was going on with me. It became apparent that Carrington didn't know everything—she had never heard of the Scepter of the Seven—but they are on my side because it was Carrington who gave me the Digglewip!

I sit up, wiping my face. "It's alright, Queen Mother. Really. What time is it? I need to get back." I get up and grab my things.

"Yes, of course. Please, Maggie. Let's see each other one-on-one often. You need someone to help you through this, and I will do my best."

"I'd love to, Queen Mother." I start to the door but pause. Something tells me to turn around and go back to Stiorri. *She saw the tree...*

I take Stiorri's hands and lean in so close that I know she now feels my breath on her cheek. "I did see Pippin, but I must go."

Queen Mother Stiorri gasps as I hurry back to my dormitory.

Chapter 8
Whitescales

That night, after another joyless feast with Thorn and Tritch, I head to the Nobility Lounge to stay away from Thorn as much as I'm allowed. When I arrive, It's clear that many other students didn't want to go back to their dormitories either. All of the sofas, armchairs, and chaise lounges are full of royals playing games or chatting amongst themselves until curfew. I notice a few unfortunate friends trying to do homework. Nathaniel Youngblood was writing a paper until he finally had enough of getting bumped. Huffing, he packs up his quill, ink, and parchment and shuffles out of the Nobility Lounge.

To my delight, Fletcher sits at a table playing chess with none other than *Ernie* who is dressed head-to-toe in royal attire!

With no chairs available, I stand at their chess table. "Hi, Fletcher. Ernie!"

Fletcher waves without looking up from the game. Ernie smiles. "Hey, Maggie."

Neither of us says anything about the Six, the Boggletrice Company, or any of it. I know better, and Ernie has obviously been coached as to what to say and what not to say here at Emily. I look to Fletcher who has a white dragon on the sash across his chest. Ernie has one too.

"Ah, Whitescale. Your love of weather," I say to Ernie knowingly.

"Yeah, I guess so," he replies bashfully.

"Did you get enough to eat?"

"Did I?" Ernie breathes. He has lived alone for years not eating much of anything, partly due to not having much food around, and partly because he couldn't stomach it after tragically losing his family in a fire he caused.

"Well, the food's usually a lot better."

"Really? I thought it was great."

Anything is great when you're starving.

"The feasts are one of the perks of living here," I say. "Are you two the same age?"

Fletcher and Ernie nod. "We are," says Ernie. "Dormmates."

"You're kidding! Fletcher, have you not had a dormmate this whole time?"

Fletcher, a man of few words, replies, "Had one. He's gone."

"Where did he go?" I ask.

Fletcher shrugs.

"Well, if you need anything, I'm in the girl's hall of Firebreather. Don't hesitate to come get me."

Ernie being here is definitely part of a Boggletrice Company plan, but how am I supposed to know what that plan is if we aren't able to talk to each other without the castle hearing?

I stand awkwardly, watching the two nine-year-olds playing chess because this is better than going to my dormitory where Thorn awaits. But after what seems like an hour but is only twenty minutes, I tell the boys goodnight. "Let's play chess each evening, okay, boys?" I say, and they both agree.

I leave the Nobility Lounge to head back to my dormitory. No one stops to talk to me or waves or anything. Not only am I no longer Head of Castle and, therefore, unworthy of the royal's praise, but I am still on the bad side of many students because of my actions at the Em Games. Not only did I beat Monika Spivey senseless due to a misunderstanding of the rules of Gottfrig's Grab, but many refused to believe me when I spilled the truth to the whole academy about how Emily actually gets its magic.

Even though I am dressed royally like everyone else, I've got no friends here, and I'm an outcast yet again. I used to think having the same clothes as everyone else would make me fit in, but I was wrong. You have to *be* like everyone else too. Maybe not on the outside, but on the inside, I'm still "Shaggy Maggie."

I drag my feet, walking as slowly as possible back to Firebreather Hall. Einsreich litter the castle, and no Snickerlings are soaring the air, only walking. Magnus is nowhere to be found, nor is Felixus. Do they even know I'm here? They must.

"Ow!"

A scroll, rolled up and tied with a purple ribbon, drops on my head and then falls at my feet. Holding my head that doesn't hurt—it just startled me badly—I look up just in time to see an owl fly out of one of the uppermost windows.

Felixus!

I scurry to get the scroll that he dropped. I don't know what's in it, but I know I don't want anyone to see it. Where can I go to read it? Definitely not my dormitory. Honestly, I don't want to open it here either for any other students to possibly see. I scan the area for a secluded spot. The loo? Maybe. I head downstairs toward the girl's bathroom by the Remembering Hall. The vast entrance hall looks naked without its blanket of Snickerlings. As I am about to pass a female Einsreich into the girl's bathroom, I hear a door open and shut as Disha Chopra emerges from the Releasing Chamber.

Why have I not thought of this before? Ignatius! I zoom into the little booth with the picture of the burning candle swallowing a snake on the door. I close the latch and sit in front of the candle the size of an average Christmas tree.

The flame bursts into being and gasps. "Princess! What are you doing here?"

"I had to come see you! I was hoping you could tell me what the others are up to?"

"This is not wise, Princess. I am to report to the Head of Academy each night. This new one, Klauschwitz, I think he's starting to suspect that I am not entirely truthful with him. I am to meet with him soon. You must go and do not come back to me again while you are here. It's too risky."

"Ignatius, Felixus just dropped this off to me. It must be a letter from the Company. I didn't want to open it where anyone might see it."

Ignatius gives an exasperated huff. "Oh, alright. Be quick! There isn't much time, and I'm afraid I, too, am being watched by this administration."

"I'll be fast," I say, pulling the purple ribbon and unrolling the scroll for Ignatius and me to see.

"Ah! Wonderful!" Ignatius exclaims quietly. "King McShanihan has sent the Digglewip. It will aid you greatly, Princess. Be sure to keep it hidden well. No one else will be able to view it unless their heart is in the right place, but you can never be too careful."

"No, I can't be too careful. I don't want to lose it," I reply, rolling the Digglewip up and putting it away in my satchel.

"You must go now, and remember, do not come back unless it is a dire emergency," Ignatius warns.

"Alright, Ignatius. See you."

I exit the Releasing Chamber and climb the stairs to Firebreather Hall. Receiving the Digglewip has made my heart heavier than it has been yet. The only way I know that it is, in fact, the magical map is because Ignatius said so. I saw only a blank scroll.

Chapter 9
Verecundiam

"Maggie!" someone whispers.

"Maggie!" This voice is Eve's.

"Maggie, over here!" Justice's voice exclaims.

Everything is pitch black. I am walking but have no clue what is under, over, or around me.

"Over here, Mags! Where are you going?" shouts Flori.

"Flori!" I cry. "Justice! Where are you all? I can't see!"

"Whatever do you mean, Princess? We're right here. Come now," Sara Lisa states plainly.

"Where?" I'm so frustrated.

"Over here!"

"I can't see! Where are you?"

"We mustn't yell, darling," says Eve.

"Sorry. It's too dark to see you all. I can't see anything!" My hands are out in front of me. I stumble into things, knocking over some of them.

"You've got to watch out, Maggie. If that were a snake it would have bitten you," Soleil giggles.

I hear squealing and squeaking buzzing by.

"Magnus, help! Shine your light so I can see!" But the pig only squeaks sadly. Soft hooting flies overhead. "Felixus! Help me!" But the owl does not come to my aid. I drop to my knees and cover my face. "I don't know what's happening. Where are we?"

"Silly girl, when will you grow up?" says George. "We're in Brumbletide, of course."

Dread sinks into my belly. I get up and stumble forward. I feel a wall and feel around until I feel a ledge. It must be the castle's front balcony. I hoist myself over the ledge to get back to Emily but no snow blusters me away like it's supposed to. I fall through blackness until I hit a wall of water, the Lux Sea.

Down, down, down, I sink.

"Maggie!"

"I can't see! I can't see!"

"Then open your eyes, stupid."

I open my eyes. Thorn is standing at the side of my bed ready for school. She is dressed in red with a ruby-pointed crown. A different Snickerling has brought us breakfast today.

"You can't be late. My dad will check to ensure you are where you're supposed to be."

"I'm not where I'm supposed to be."

Thorn ignores my comment. "Don't be late."

I sit up and rub my eyes. "Alright, where am I going first?"

"Hanging Gardens," the Snickerling tells me, handing me a

coffee with a lid.

"Thank you. Thorn, I'll be on my way as soon as I'm dressed."

"Be quick. I'm telling you; he's watching." Thorn grabs her satchel and leaves the dormitory for class.

I do a quick washup, and the Snickerling helps me put on a beautiful feathery, white dress that reminds me much of her wings.

"Have you replaced Jericho?" I ask the Snickerling girl.

"Oh, no one can replace Jericho, my lady. Just filling in while she's away, is all."

"What's your name?"

"Evangeline."

"What a beautiful name."

"Why thank you, Princess Maggie," Evangeline replies, placing my crown on my head. The crown bonds to me, sending warm energy surging through my limbs and core. I mustn't let anyone know the obsidian has power. I must not let my memories get the best of me.

"Well, nice to meet you, Evangeline. I'll see you later. Off to Horticulture."

"See you, Princess Maggie. Have a good class," replies the Snickerling kindly.

I climb through the trunk of the mystical wisteria into the Hanging Gardens of Flori. In the magnificent gardens today, Queen Mother Hertha has set several plants in a row for us to tend.

I pray silently these plants are nothing like the vicious Mixship Skelm.

"Everyone! I have potted these verecundiams for all of you to have one. Over the next several days you will tend to your vercundiam as you will be instructed today. This plant is one of the most mysterious in all the Gardens, meaning it will be one of the most mysterious and extraordinary things you will see in your life. By the end of the week, you will be experts on this plant that while beautiful, has brought kings to their knees. Take a seat by the plant of your choice."

I sit down cross-legged by the smallest one I can find. The verecundiam is a silvery leafy plant with no flowers. Seems harmless enough.

"Now class, the verecundiam may seem to you like a regular old house plant, but I assure you it is anything but. Lean in close to the leaves."

Everyone bows their heads close to their plant. Making sure not to take my eyes off it, I bring my face close to the silvery leaves, bracing myself to flee at the first sign of movement. But there is no movement. The plant is completely still. A quiet hissing comes forth. I feel air on my face. "You cannot see the kingdom," comes a chilling whisper.

I gasp and recoil. Looking around, the other students are staring at their plants uneasily as well.

Queen Mother Hertha watches us all. "You see, there is more than meets the eye when it comes to the verecundiam. Water your plant three times daily, and feed it junk food at least once daily."

"Junk food? How do we feed it junk food?" asks Eden Kung.

"Bury it in its soil. You can use any junk, but in my experience, it likes sugar and white flour best."

Trumpets blast.

"Until we meet again, your majesties! Good luck with this one," Queen Mother Hertha's expression softens, and she clasps her hands. Her shoulders loosen as if she is taking off her hat of instruction and putting on her hat of empathy. "Let it not overcome you, children."

I carry the verecundiam as far from my face as I can get it. I don't know which is worse, the Mixship Skelm that could rip my face off or this.

"The kingdom is dead to you," it hisses. I lift the plant above my head, holding it high in the air, and walk as fast as my legs will go up the heavenly staircase to Firebreather Hall. I will not carry this thing around all day. I burst into the room and set the verecundiam in the corner far away from my bed. To my horror, another verecundiam is on Thorn's desk.

"You will never save anyone now," mine jeers.

"Shut up!" I snap at the plant and hurry out of the room.

But just before I close the door, "You *would* tell a plant to shut up."

I slam the door and run to catch a runaway carpet to Soleil Tower. As I cross the hall, I feel a tug on my dress and whip around to see Ernie! He hands me a folded note and keeps walking.

Good job, Ernie.

I jump and hang on for dear life to a carpet holding Missy Orr and Eden Kung. They help me onto the carpet, and we all work to keep each other from falling off.

"Where are you going, Maggie?" asks Eden, panting.

"Soleil Tower."

"Us too! Aaaaaah!" shouts Missy as the carpet tries to buck us off. "Grip the edge, Maggie! It *will* throw you off."

We are dumped into the medieval classroom at the top of Soleil Tower and land with a thud amongst the experimental beds with shackles and switches on the wall that never seem to stop popping and cracking. When everyone is present, Queen Mother Felberta leads us down to the tower's first floor, which is a vast lecture hall. Good, I'll be able to read Ernie's note here.

I sit by Eden and Missy in the lecture hall. The two of them have no shortage of questions for me.

"What the heck is going on around here, Maggie? You've got to know. You were Head of Castle, after all!" Eden whispers pretty loudly. "Who are all these weird kids? Or *what* are these weird kids? And what happened to you? You were here. You were a Daughter of Eve. You were Head of Castle! Then you were gone. Then you were back. Now Thorn is Head of Castle, and all this strange stuff is happening. Blimey!"

"It all makes me super anxious," says Missy. "I want to send a letter to Mum."

"Can we mail letters?" I ask.

"Yes, there's a post office in The Resplendent. I haven't sent a letter yet, but I've seen postal cottage."

"I never noticed it in The Resplendent," says Eden. "I'll make a point to look next time I'm there."

"You know, I think I have seen it," I say, remembering some cottages in The Resplendent we never visited. I paid little attention because we didn't go to them for our fitting.

"What's going on here, Maggie?" Eden asks again, urgently this time.

"I'm not allowed to say."

Eden and Missy don't respond but their expressions are full of frustration and anxiousness. I wish I could say something, but I can't risk losing even the slight chance I will be able to get back to the Boggletrice Company.

Queen Mother Felberta takes her podium. "Quills ready? Lots of notes today."

We all dip our quills and get our parchment ready. Queen Mother Felberta gives us a moment before beginning her lecture.

"Alchemy," she begins.

You're kidding.

"Alchemy, the ancient practice of recreating precious materials from common materials. Founded by Democritus in 460 BCE, the study and practice of alchemy continued into the 1700s when it was allegedly proven false and replaced by chemistry." Queen Mother Felberta gives us a minute to catch up on our notes before continuing. "Let me ask you this, do you really think that alchemists devoted their life's work to a fantasy for two thousand years? They were doing nothing and passing nothing along to the future generations for *two thousand* years?"

That does sound pretty illogical. But as much as I want to listen to every word of Felberta's lecture on alchemy, I've got to read Ernie's note. Looking around for any sign of "watchers"—who or what are these watchers anyway? I don't even know what to look for—I unfold the little note.

The others said not to talk to you except when you had the Ticklewip or something. Let me know when you have it. -Ernie

My chest sinks. Miss Squaffletree worked hard to get Ernie enrolled here at Emily Academy, and now I'm useless to him because I've lost sight of Pippin and Brumbletide. I can't see the Digglewip.

For the rest of the class, I think of various ways to run away from both Emily and Little Ipswich and start a new life in a faraway elsewhere.

A frog hops onto my foot. I scream which incites Eden and Missy to scream and upset the entire lecture.

What's with these damn frogs?

Chapter 10
Hoplology Happenings

Snickerlings are busy delivering letters to all of us students, especially those of us assigned the essay on chapters one through nine in *A Tale of a King*. It is Evangeline who hands me my scroll and confiscates my book. The letter reads:

Your Fine Majesties of Emily,

It has been brought to attention that the library has been tampered with. All books are to be returned to Michelle Tower immediately, and no books will be borrowed until the issue is resolved. We apologize for this inconvenience.

Head King of Academy,

King Wilheim Klauschwitz

I shake my head. I knew they'd do something like this when they finally noticed. Looking at the signature, I think of Queen Mother Maymie, who is usually the one writing these letters as Head Queen Mother. Where is she? Was she killed after she came to the Boggletrice Company Headquarters and helped us? My throat tightens at the thought. She was so miserable. I hope she's at peace now.

High Noon Fair is miserable too. Today I spend it again with Klauschitz, Tritch, and Thorn.

"I saw your verecundiam in the dormitory, Maggie," says Thorn. "They don't like the corner. You should keep it by your bed. They enjoy human interaction."

"Absolutely not. I want the least interaction with that thing as possible! I hope it dies."

Tritch grimaces "Stupid girl. The verecundiam is an extraordinary specimen that deserves as much attention and study as we can give it. Klauschwitz and I have done extensive work with it and are constantly dumbfounded by its myriad of beneficial uses."

"I find you dumb too," I mumble without thinking.

Tritch Anguis wipes his mouth with his napkin, gets up quietly, walks to my seat, and dumps my plate of gruel in my lap. "Oh! I'm sorry, Princess!" he wails apologetically so all the students can hear him. He then bends down to me and whispers. "We will kill you when the time is right."

I roll my eyes as the Snickerlings rush to my aid.

My next class is Hoplology with Queen Mother Berthilda, but since all weapons have been deemed off-limits, we are swimming today—in February.

We were instructed to go first to The Resplendent to receive our water wear. I ride with the class on the ferry manned by the biggest Einsreich princess I've seen yet. When we reach the monstrous whirlpool, no one objects to having to jump into it. We all get our life vests on our own and jump in the Lux swiftly.

I'm sucked through the raging whirl, then swim through the teapot to the spout, where I am plunged into a teacup with Eden Kung. No one says much as we bob along the little river to The Resplendent's shore where a mix of Snickerlings and Einsreich await us.

On the way to Fit for a King, I make a point to look for the postal cottage. Aside from the salon, shoe shop, crown shop, and robes, there is a cottage called Flori's Satchel, probably where the Snickerlings make our school bags. One cottage with a ship's helm on the front called Justice at Sea is surely the place to get repair parts for the ferry, and Sara Lisa's Adornment is an accessory shop displaying jewelry, hair clips, sashes, and house badges in the window. Eve's Letters has various stationary, quills, and diaries.

Diaries! Where is Eve's diary? I can't even remember where I've seen it last! Why? *Why* am I put in charge of this stuff? I'm the worst! I've got to search for it as soon as possible.

But next to Eve's Letters, behold, a little building with several mailboxes out front that is unmistakably the postal cottage. Of course, in usual Resplendent fashion, the mailboxes are the kind on posts at the end of neighborhood driveways instead of the big metal ones at regular post offices. A sign hangs from the thatched roof that reads "The Messenger." I'll attempt to send a letter soon.

We file into Fit for a King where Snickerlings are hurriedly working to get us ready for swimming. I step in—and gasp.

"Rat," Queen Mother Maymie grunts.

Queen Mother Maymie! She's alive! Overcome with relief, I run to her and throw my arms around her thick neck to which she immediately rips me from it, sending me flying into Cecilia Hernandez. Cecilia and I tumble into the rack of long-sleeved white suits that topples over with us in it.

"How dare you touch me, Rat! Do that again, it's your head."

"What were you thinking, Maggie?" Cecilia whispers in disbelief of my actions. Snickerlings help us up and immediately hold a curtain up so we can change. The magic is gone from the curtains, so Snickerlings are the ones standing on stools and holding them for crouching students to change into their swimsuits. Somehow the mirrors still levitate.

If Queen Mother Maymie is acting, she deserves an Academy Award. Has she changed her mind? Or is she acting like that so she won't be killed? My head hurts.

When we are all suited up with swimwear that looks like white scuba suits, we all hurry to the fire in the middle of The Resplendent that takes us back to the ferry where Queen Mother Berthilda is waiting.

"Class, you will all jump in and doggy paddle until you feel the pull of the whirlpool, then flip and backstroke to the ferry. Everyone, step up on the ledge here. On my whistle…"

We all balance on the ferry's ledge. Queen Mother Berthilda blows her whistle, and we all dive into the Lux. I am not a good swimmer, so I am not completely surprised when I am pulled deep underwater because of Missy Orr and Cecilia Hernandez jumping in next to me. I am surprised, however, by the voices in the Lux!

Under the water in the watery quiet, there are voices—loud whispers like that of the verecundiam, but louder and sharper.

"Remember!"

"Remember, Maggie!"

"Remember, remember..."

"Remember!"

"Remember what?" I say, swallowing water and choking. Panicking, I get up to the surface as fast as I can. When my face hits the air, I gasp and cough. The whole class is already backstroking to the ferry. Behind, I swim the best I can, entirely forgoing the doggy paddle. I reach the pull of the whirlpool unexpectantly and am sucked into the vortex.

Chapter 11
The Messenger

In the teacup boat, I bob along, coughing and gasping, trying to regain normal breath function. There is no way back to the ferry except through The Resplendent.

The teacup bumps into the white sandy shore. There are no Snickerlings to help me; they weren't expecting anyone here at this time. Einsreich are perched like creepy wound-down toys, paying me no attention, their heads hanging in front of them, watching their feet. Soaking wet and still in my swimsuit, I walk toward the village fire, the way back to the ferry.

Something about being out of class when no one else is always makes me linger a little longer than necessary. And it is this lingering that has me noticing the other cottages I've never been to. There is the postal cottage! I can't help myself, I must go in. Will I really be able to send a letter to the Boggletrice Company telling them what has happened?

The welcoming crimson door jingles when I open it. Inside the small cottage, a birdcage containing a raven and an owl (not Felixus) hangs behind the desk. An armchair is situated by the fire, and tea and a stack of books are on the table next to it. Everywhere else are mailboxes.

There are red mailboxes with black flags, checked ones with windows, brick ones like that of a wealthy manor, mailboxes shaped like carriages and houses, and even plain ole black ones. This is the post office? And just as I am wondering where the postman is, a small back door opens and in walks—walks on two feet now—a badger about the size of Mrs. Cloudt but thicker. He wears round spectacles on his black and white face and is dressed in a soft, green sweater. He whistles a tune.

"Ah, who do we have here?" he says upon seeing me. "Going for a swim?"

He talks too! "Well, sir, I was swimming and wound up here accidentally."

"I see," the badger says curiously. "It is interesting all the ways this place is found. Job found it in his mother-in-law's house. Horatio Spafford found it in a pig pen. Queen Victoria was on a wayward horse that took her to a dime shop. And C.S. Lewis found it in the bathroom of a pub. You were swimming. Ha! I am amused."

"Doesn't everyone who wants to send a letter find the post office?" I ask. Now I am the curious one.

The badger raises a finger. "Certainly."

"Then what do you mean, sir?"

The owl and raven rustle in their cage.

"Now, now, men, I haven't forgotten." The badger pulls some bugs out of his pocket and pokes them through the cage. "Carriers," smiles the badger. "They like this cage. I try letting them roam free when they aren't working, but they are both such homebodies. Strange creatures."

I can't help but think that the badger himself is a strange creature.

The badger whistles softly. "If one wants to mail a letter, they certainly go to the post office. But if one is receiving a message, they come here." He lifts his paws to the room around him. He then searches the slew of mailboxes and opens a bright blue one with a cardinal on top. Its red flag is raised. "And here we are. Your message." The badger brings me the contents of the mailbox, a letter with a purple wax seal. I take it, but I have some questions before opening it.

"You mean this office is only for people receiving messages? How are they supposed to know they have one? I came here by accident."

The badger looks at me out the top of his spectacles. "Seems an accident, but everyone who has a message here finds their way. Now, I would read it if I were you. Everyone receives their message right on time, but you must open it."

Speechless, I open the letter addressed to:

Princess Maggie Prewitt

Soaking Wet in The Resplendent

Emily Castle, Little Ipswich

It has been sent "Royal Mail" but there is no return address. I try to keep the purple wax seal intact. It has the crest of a shield, crowns, candles, and a winged pig. *Pippin? Is this from you? Or who?*

I carefully remove the heavy paper. The letter is written in elegant calligraphy like the ones from Emily, but somehow, I can tell this is not from anyone at the castle.

What if it never happened? Think. Remember. What if it never happened? Some things are never stirred if not shaken first. You will never receive all the details you'd like. You do not need them. Think. Remember. What if it never happened?

The badger closes the mailbox and sits down in front of the fire. He opens a book. "I won't be seeing you again. It was a pleasure."

"Why will you not see me again? What if I get another message?"

"Messages like these come very rarely. Many never receive even one. Those who find this place have experienced a great tragedy, so a message is given. Most need to go finding their messages elsewhere. Good luck! Good day!" he waves over his shoulder. Pushing up his glasses, he gets into his book.

I glance around the cottage, which now seems more mysterious and peculiar than ever.

"Good day, sir," I say. The door jingles again as I exit to go back to the fire. I read the message over and over again on the way. What does it mean? Remember what? This is so frustrating!

THE MESSENGER

I walk into the fire, and when I appear in the oven of the ferry. I step out to see everyone seated in the nooks, bundled in towels and eating refreshments.

"There she is!" exclaims Queen Mother Berthilda huskily. "Need some practice with that doggy paddle. It's what slows ya down so you can sense the whirlpool coming and avoid it. But glad ya made it back, Princess. She wraps a fluffy towel around my shoulders. "Have a seat. Class is almost dismissed."

I sit bewildered in a nook next to Missy Orr. "Are you alright, Maggie?" she asks.

"Yes," I say. "Found the postal cottage. You've got a massage there."

Chapter 12
Doomed

Sitting with the Anguises and Klauschwitz at the evening feast, I am so lonely in a room of hundreds. Not only is the feast the worst it's been yet, just pots of gruel and mystery stew, but the Snickerlings brought word that we were to bring our verecundiams so that we could feed them. In addition to the mysterious, soggy mush, there are piles of convenience store candy, crisps, and biscuits that most kids choose to eat instead of the feast. I set my verecundiam with Thorn and ignore her when she tries to tell me to feed it.

Again today, Klauschwitz stands at the podium and wonkily addresses us through the Einsreich.

"Fi-fine young roy-aaaaals of Em-Emily, I want to say that I-I-I appreciaaaaaate your welcoming our neeeeew students more this weeeeeeek. In order to be be be be more inclusive, royals will be be be be expected to call the Infernum stu-students 'Your Maaaaaajesty' as well as 'Priiii-iiiince' and 'Princesseeeeess.' The

Infernum trans-transfers deserve the titles just as much as yoooooouuuu ah-aaaall, and from now on, you as ac-ac-academy students will beeeee ex-expected to address them as such. The Queen-Queen Mothers have beeeeen instructed to reprimand and demerit anyone who who who isn't act-acting accordingly. Again, awkwardness and even discomfort are expected at at at fiiiiirrrrrst. All of you fine rooooooyals of Emily have lived pri-pri-privileged lives surrounded by people ju-just like your-yourselves. It it it it is tiiiiiime to progress.

"Love. When yoooooouuuu fee-feel uncomfortable, remem-mem-mem-member, all in the naaaaame of love." Without saying anything else, Klauschwitz walks out of the Throne Room, and the carpets of doom come to take the royals, many screaming in terror, to their destinations. Thorn and I are already on the floor and opt to walk. I didn't want to walk with Thorn, but here she is.

"Going back to the dormitory, Maggie?"

"No, I was going to the Nobility Lounge. That plant is hideous." *AND I DON'T WANT TO BE ALONE WITH YOU*. Though I didn't say the words out loud, I get the feeling that Thorn knows what I wanted to say.

"Well, I'm going to the room. Don't forget to feed your verecundiam." She puts some candy in my satchel before I can protest.

"Mine's on a diet," I tell Thorn bluntly.

"Maggie, I know you don't like all the changes, and you don't trust my dad—"

"Hmm, wonder why that might be. Why wouldn't I trust

your dad?" I put my finger to my chin. "Oh, that's right, he locked my friends and me in the dungeon and left us for dead. And let's see, oh yeah, he kidnapped me and brought me here against my will and said he's only keeping me alive for now so no one asks too many questions. Seems like there's something else, doesn't it?"

"Maggie."

"Oh! He brought an entire army of zombie kids here and now makes us bow to them. The list goes on, but that's a banger of a start wouldn't you say?" Furious, I stomp off to the Nobility Lounge leaving Thorn standing there. *Why is she being nice to me?*

"You are a death omen to this institution," the verecundiam hisses.

"I'm glad!" I snap.

Fletcher and Ernie are back at the chess table in the Nobility Lounge. They both have verecundiams sitting at their feet. *Oh no, Ernie!*

When Ernie looks up at me from his game, he is stark white.

"Ernie, are you alright? Do not listen to *anything* that thing says. It's a wicked creature."

"It's all true what it says," Ernie croaks. "I killed them all. Why'd I ever leave Dragon Street? I belong in jail!"

Fletcher gives a sideways glance at Ernie saying this, but he too has a long face likely due to his verecundiam's verbal assaults.

I pick up both of the boy's plants that spit and chant rude comments all the way to the fireplace that I set them down by. I set my own there, too, fighting the urge to throw them all in. "Your dad is dead because of *you*. Because of *you!*"

I swat the plant. It screams. It takes all I have not to toss them all into the fire, but I don't want to get Ernie, of all people, in trouble.

Back at the chess table, Ernie and Fletcher are both hunched over with their fists to their temples.

"Boys, do not, I repeat, do *not* listen to those plants. Stay away from them as much as you can. All they spew is hideous lies!"

"But—" starts Ernie.

I put my finger to his lips and lower my voice. "Lies. You know the truth, Ernie. You did not murder anyone. This project can't be over fast enough. Why would they give us such an awful assignment?" But even as I say the words, I know. Two people: Klauschwitz and Anguis. But why?

Fists still to his temples, Ernie asks quietly, "Did you find the diggle-thing, Maggie?"

My cheeks burn. Ernie's words are worse than anything the verecundiam has said yet. "Er, not yet. I have to figure a few things out. I'll let you know as soon as possible, I promise."

Ernie nods and moves his pawn. Embarrassed, I decide to go back to the dormitory after all. I bid Fletcher and Ernie goodbye, reminding them to stay away from the verecundiam and head to Firebreather Hall.

Do you ever get the feeling you're being watched? I have that feeling currently, but I really am almost constantly being watched, so hopefully that's all the feeling is. The dragons of

Firebreather Hall breathe their fire, and I jump as usual. I will never get used to them.

"Maggie," someone whispers.

I look around. There are other princesses in Firebreather Hall, but none of them look like they just said something to me.

"Maggie," the voice comes from behind the statue of Michelle that stands in the middle of the corridor. Slowly, I step toward it. There is no one around it.

I look at Michelle in his wicked, smirking, face and, looking this way and that, whisper, "Did you say my name?"

"MAGGIE!" Thorn pushes me hard. She and I fall forward as the candlelit chandelier above crashes to the floor. The carpet goes up in flames—real flames, not Ignatius flames. The hall is catching fire before our eyes.

"Run!" I yell.

Students are running and screaming. Snickerlings, too, are panicking, grabbing students by the arms and hurrying them out of Firebreather Hall. They have no way of putting it out without their magic except conventional methods. Einsreich are present but do nothing. We all run to the Remembering Hall while more Snickerlings bring buckets and buckets of water. Alarmed by the screaming, every student and Queen Mother has now come to see what's happening. I start to panic with claustrophobia crowded by royals and smoke billowing overhead. There's no way for all of us to escape except by taking the ferry or diving into the Lux. We all watch nervously as Snickerlings bravely run into Firebreather Hall with water and then quickly out again to fetch more. The stupid Einsrech still do nothing.

Finally, the fire is out after hundreds of buckets of water, but Firebreather Hall is unlivable. Klauschwitz informs us that Firebreathers will be dispersed in other halls until our dormitories are restored, and we are to wait for the Queen Mothers to take us to where we will stay.

I huddle by Thorn, hugging myself, trying not to hyperventilate. I want to push everyone away. Thorn, of all people, just saved my life from probably her own family. My things have all burned including the Digglewip and Eve's diary. Leave it to me to destroy two things that have remained intact for over seven hundred years. If it wasn't clear before, we are all doomed.

Yet, as a poopy lining to it all, my verecundiam is still in my hands, safe and sound. "You'd be better off dead!"

Chapter 13
Clair Shelley

Klauschwitz has all royals return to their dormitories except us Firebreathers and the Queen Mothers. The Queen Mother assigned to bring Thorn and I to our new living quarters is Queen Mother Felberta of Whitescale House. She approaches us uneasily. This isn't only because of the fire. Felberta was recently possessed by none other than Michelle himself when given a ruby crown as a gift from Thorn. I know she would like to say something to me because she was with us when Pippin brought Calysta back to life after being turned to stone by Medusa, but she doesn't dare with Thorn present.

"Come along, girls." Queen Mother Felberta says, leading us to Whitescale Hall at the other end of the castle. Two white dragons stand watch at this hall but have smoke billowing from their nostrils instead of fire like the Firebreather dragons.

Every house hall has empty dormitories in it. We walk the corridor to the white drawbridge-like door. No names appear anywhere because of the lack of Snickerling magic. Felberta removes a key from her pocket and unlocks the drawbridge. It slowly falls open to a spectacular suite with a real night sky for a ceiling. Flames hang over oak desks with globes, compasses, and hourglasses. Wes will hate that he wasn't placed in Whitescale!

Thorn walks in and immediately begins unpacking her satchel onto the desk.

"Snickerlings will brings your clothes and toiletries. Make yourself at home, princesses."

"Thank you, Queen Mother," I reply.

Felberta looks at me, then at Thorn, then at me again. I can tell she wants to tell me something but can't.

"Queen Mother, I'll see you in your class tomorrow," I say.

Felberta's eyes brighten. "Very good. You girls sleep well." The door lifts and begins to close on its own, but before it is fully shut, it lowers again. A girl our age with white hair and a playful smirk breezes in. There is something strange about her though. She looks like one of us, but not. Her white gown is beautiful, but I've not seen that particular style worn by any of the girls yet. It has an empire waist and oversized puffy sleeves like something out of the Renaissance. But her face. I wonder if she has an illness. She has dark circles under her eyes and is very pale. Despite this, she is very peppy and forward.

"Hello, neighbors," she chirps. "I'm in the dormitory next door." She holds her hand out to Thorn, who doesn't take it. Without missing a beat, the girl swings around to me and offers the secondhand hand. "Clair. Clair Shelley."

I do shake her hand, which is very cold. "Pleasure," I reply, amused.

"It's almost curfew, Clair Shelley," says Thorn. "Best be getting back to your dormitory. Your dormmate may be lonely."

At this, Clair Shelley shakes her head and narrows her eyes. "No dormmate. Had one, but she's gone now." She eyes Thorn as if she should know precisely what Clair is talking about. Thorn ignores her and continues putting her things away.

"No idea what's happened to her, hmm?" Clair Shelley stares at Thorn even more intensely. Her smirk is gone.

"How long has she been missing?" I ask.

Clair sits in one of the armchairs. Thorn rolls her eyes.

"Been a while now. I've been unable to shake the feeling that this girl's lot's behind it." She thumbs over at Thorn.

"Last time I checked, talking that way about a Head of Castle merits a trip to the dungeon," Thorn says calmly.

Clair's smirk returns. "Fine. My dormmate was a good student, smart as a whip. But she came to Emily from Dragon Street. Got a scholarship and was able to attend the academy of her dreams. First one ever to attend the academy in her long line of poverty-stricken family. Now she's gone, and there are others missing too—all from Dragon Street, the slums of town."

I think of Ernie, whom we brought from Dragon Street, and shudder. How have I missed this happening here?

Clair gets up, walks to Thorn, and sets her face almost nose to nose with her. "Seems real strange, right? No one from Victor's

Spoil is missing. Not one. All from Dragon Street. *Real* strange."

The old Thorn resurrects, and she hisses and bites at Clair who recoils. "I don't know what you're talking about, but I do know I can have you removed from here and punished however I see fit."

Clair laughs and goes to the door. "Something's up, and it has to do with you and your dad. I *will* find out what." She winks at me and exits our dormitory. The door doesn't close on its own, so Thorn pulls it to. She returns to her things like nothing happened.

"What was that about?" I ask. "Is your dad kicking off poor people?"

"No, of course not."

"Of course not? *Of course* that seems like something he would do."

"Maggie, tuition is tuition. He doesn't care where it comes from. No Emily Head of Castle has ever cared where it comes from."

"I would have."

Thorn gives me an almost sympathetic look that clearly states I am not counted as one of the Emily Heads of Castle.

A Snickerling comes in bringing our pajamas and more gowns. Thorn and I change and get into the white yet heavily gothic beds. I don't question Thorn anymore, but I will most definitely question Clair Shelley in the morning. I roll over onto my side. The verecundiam hisses, "You will do nothing! You've lost sight!"

"Dammit, Thorn! I told you I didn't want this thing by the bed!"

The verecundiam screams as I carry it to the desk. Huffing, I curl up in my covers and try to sleep.

In the morning, Snickerlings apologetically serve us cold gruel and help us dress for the day. Thorn's first class is Horticulture, so she feeds her verecundiam a lollipop and heads to class. But before she leaves, she reminds me to feed my mine, advising me to bring the plant to all my classes today.

"Absolutely not," I reply bluntly.

The Snickerling dresses me in a lovely, flowing white gown and places my crown on my head. My skin tingles when it makes contact. I breathe a little sigh of relief at choosing to keep the obsidian in my girdle as it could have been lost in the fire! I will not make the mistake of leaving it unattended like I did the diary, which is now a bunch of ashes. My stomach sinks at yet another epic failure.

I bid the Snickerling farewell, but since she can't fly, she walks with me out of the dormitory. Clair Shelley's visit last night comes to mind, and I check the next door for her name. Nothing shows up. I keep forgetting the Snickerling magic is gone.

"Ping, do you know the girl who lives in this room? She said her name was Clair Shelley, I think."

The little Snickerling girl—this one has light tan skin and almond eyes—looks at me curiously. "No one lives in that dormitory, ma'am. Hasn't for years. Clair Shelley, I remember her, but she died about forty years ago."

I stare at the Snickerling as ice enters my veins. "Are you sure? She just visited us last night. She was grilling Thorn about possibly knowing what happened to her dormmate. She said she had disappeared."

The Snickerling's little eyes are wide—very wide. "Princess Maggie, I believe you've seen a ghost. I've been at Emily three hundred years. I remember Clair Shelley—vibrant fighter of a girl. Her dormmate disappeared—there were several disappearing at that time. Very strange. Princess Clair Shelley was not settling for the answers she was getting from the Head of Academy and Queen Mothers. She let her thoughts be known. Loudly. To everyone. Many students started to believe her." The Snickerling's little black pig tails droop. "It wasn't long before Clair Shelley became one of the missing."

Speechless, all I can muster is, "Thank you, Ping."

"You are welcome, Princess. Please, if you see Princess Clair Shelley again, give her my kind regards. I always enjoyed her."

"I will," I reply breathlessly.

I am sad there will be no Atticus or Calysta in any of my classes today, but I am thrilled that my first class is Non-Common Sense with Queen Mother Stiorri. When I reach the top of the long corkscrew staircase, Queen Mother Stiorri is standing at the door greeting me with a big smile. I am immediately warmed.

"Hello, Princess." Stiorri stops me before I enter the classroom. "I requested to be your first class today and explained that you need extra care. Please stay after class for a short time." She smiles warmly.

"Yes, Queen Mother." I want to tell her about Clair Shelley, but how do I fit it in with everything else there is to talk about?

I walk into a whole class of downcast faces. There are several verecundiams screaming and hissing at their owners. I find a secluded desk on the far side of the tower and sit at it. Missy Orr is in tears. Eden Kung actually slaps his plant. When everyone is seated, Queen Mother Stiorri takes a look at her class, and her face falls. "Oh, dear. Looks like our lesson will be changing today. We need to discuss how to combat verbal abuse."

Chapter 14
I Believe You

Queen Mother Stiorri's lesson in Non-Common Sense proved invaluable against the terrible verecundiams. But the comfort was short-lived, as I remembered that Horticulture was next on today's class schedule, and we would be tending to the wretched plants. Luckily, I will be late because of Queen Mother Stiorri's request to talk to me after her class.

I keep my seat as the other royals get up to leave. I watch as Cecilia Hernandez examines the strap of her satchel and breathes a sigh of relief at finding it intact.

When everyone is gone, Queen Mother Stiorri brings a quill and ink and quietly but swiftly moves a desk to face mine. "Let's start the journey to healing, shall we?" She says this seriously but winks discreetly letting me know there is more to this exercise than meets the eye.

"Since we do not have much time, I will only ask you two questions when we meet like this. The work will be silent. I will write you one question; you will write me the answer. Then we will wad it up and throw it into the fire." She indicates the crackling blaze in the fireplace. "Then we'll do the whole thing one more time. You'll understand more of why we're doing this exercise as we go through it."

"Alright, Queen Mother."

Queen Mother Stiorri dips the quill into the black ink and writes something on the parchment. She is taking longer than I thought as she is supposedly only writing one question. When she has finished, she slides the parchment to me. It reads, *"This pertains to what we spoke of the other day. If you do not trust me yet, I certainly understand. You do not have to answer. I would like to ask a million questions but unfortunately, I cannot because we are being closely watched, my dear. Are the Einsreich and the change in administration part of some wicked plot? Is this the fulfillment of the Foxenbrand prophecy?"*

Technically, that's two questions, but it's okay. I write, *"Yes, they are all part of a wicked plot. No, that prophecy was fulfilled when Michelle built Emily seven hundred years ago."* I slide the parchment back to Stiorri who reads my words with furrowed brows. She shakes her head as if they must be incorrect, but she composes herself and slides the paper back. "Alright, princess. Crumple up the paper and throw it into the fire." She hands me the parchment and I do as she says. But when I throw the wad into the fire, it whispers, "Oh, I will go so it will burn. See you!" Ignatius leaves and the parchment is black ashes in no time. It feels good. The secret Stiorri and I have shared is now just between us.

I BELIEVE YOU

When I sit back down, Queen Mother Stiorri has already written something on another parchment. "That was only a warm-up. This will be more healing. Healing is not to be confused with comforting, mind you."

When she slides the parchment to me, I read silently, *"What is the most shame you have ever felt?"*

It doesn't take long to think of. Even though I have humiliated myself time and time again, one thing is the worst in my mind. I write, *"Leaving my little brother at home with our awful mother while I ran away to find our dad who left her."* Tears fill my eyes. *"Then our dad died because Emily poisoned him by mistake instead of me. I never thought of my brother until the funeral. I feel awful."* I slide the paper back and watch Queen Mother Stiorri try to hold back shock as she reads. Her browns stay furrowed, yet her eyes speak volumes. They then soften with sadness and meet mine. Her expression discloses utter sympathy as well as utter concern. She frantically writes on the parchment, and when it is passed back, it reads, *"My darling,"* she sounds like Eve. *"I believe you but am in pure shock at your words. You must forgive my inability to respond thoroughly immediately. As for your brother, listen closely. You are a young girl. Despite all the grown-up things you have been through in recent months, you can only work with the tools you currently have in your thirteen-year-old mind. And for what it's worth, most adults would do the same thing you did. This one will take a few times of throwing it away in order to move forward, but give yourself grace, Love."*

"Now, crumple it up, Princess Maggie," Stiorri says aloud, "and toss it in the fire. Release yourself from it. There is peace in the present; consider how your brother is today."

I nod and do as I am told. I think Queen Mother Stiorri is right in that it will take a few times before this exercise works, but watching the parchment erupt into flames and turn to ash does, in fact, make me feel a little bit better. A little bit lighter.

Queen Mother Stiorri meets me in front of the fire and takes my hands. "Until next time, my darling. Focus on the present. Remember there is peace in the present, and the present is what is real. Even if everything is in disarray, it is never as bad as what our minds project. But when you do slip into the past, which I'm sure you will, remember the good. There is always good to be found there."

There it is again—*remember*.

Queen Mother Stiorri gives me a big hug and whispers in my ear, "I believe you." Then she bids me farewell.

I descend the winding staircase with so much hope that I'm trembling. I do not mind nearly as much now that I must retrieve my verecundiam for Horticulture. On the way to Whitescale Hall, I receive a mix of thumbs-ups, high fives, scowls, and eye rolls, but I am not fazed. What does slow my steps, however—stops me right in my tracks—is the door just before mine and Thorn's. It is the supposed door of Clair Shelley and her missing dormmate. The empty dormitory where no one lives—no one *alive*. I stand staring at the white drawbridge door. There is a brass eighteen over it. Dormitory eighteen. How funny, Miss Squaffletree's office in

I BELIEVE YOU

Little Ipswich Library is also room eighteen. I do not know what propels me to do it, but I turn the knob and the drawbridge lowers. It isn't locked. Slowly and apprehensively, as if I will suddenly see the bodies of Clair and her dormmate, I pull down the door that creeks a bit as it lowers. Inside, the dormitory has all the same furnishings as our room, but it is cold, lacking life. I step to the beds and then to a desk. I'm not sure what I think I'll find but I am looking for something. *Something.*

"Hello, again."

I trip over the armchair, falling into the desk, knocking over a globe.

"I'd help you, but I can't pick it up." Clair Shelley bends down and swipes her hand through the globe. "Still, forty years later, I can't figure it out. Some things I can touch, some things I can't."

"You're—you're a ghost," I stutter.

"Not quite. I am a memory that refuses to die."

"A memory?"

"Yes. That's what we call it anyway. Over the years, we've gathered that Michelle's spirit lives on in those loyal to Emily. There is something that lives on in those that hate it as well."

"W-We?" I breathe.

Clair Shelley gives a genuine smile realizing this must be too much for me. "Meet me in the dungeon tonight after the feast. I'll tell you more there."

"But there is no way I'll be able to get down to the dungeon tonight. They're watching me like hawks around here."

"You will. I promise you will." Clair becomes translucent and slowly fades away. "Don't worry. You will. Just go there tonight."

I watch the place where Clair Shelley once was for several seconds before moving. Trumpets blast, startling me, and I hurry to get my verecundiam and then race to Horticulture.

The hideous plant hisses horrid phrases to me the whole way to the mystical wisteria of the Hanging Gardens. "Lies! Lies! She tells you a myriad of lies. You are so stupid. Of course you believe her."

Chapter 15
Funny HaHa

"Shut up!" I spit to the verecundiam as I crawl through the trunk of the glittering wisteria.

"Hypocrite," the plant mumbles.

The class is seated on the grassy knoll before Queen Mother Hertha. Every single royal has a long face. Eden Kung even has his hands over his ears.

"These things are worse than the Mixship Skelms, Queen Mother," says Missy Orr sitting a great distance away from her plant.

"Certainly so," replies Queen Mother Hertha. "But I've always quite enjoyed the Mixship Skelm—a fascinating creature. The verecundiam, however, has more cons than pros. Strange, too, is that we haven't dealt with this particular plant in years. The current administration specifically requested that it become a large part of our curriculum. I'm so sorry, students. Hopefully, we can get through this year unscathed."

The class moans. No one is unscathed. Like Missy, I set down my verecundiam and sit several feet away from it.

"Alright, class, the verecundiam is a unique species of the genus Dionaea, which means 'petite dragon.' Unlike the Mixship Skelm of the same genus, the verecundiam is not carnivorous in the same sense. The verecundiam feeds off souls and grows more voracious with junk food."

I will not be feeding it ever again!

But Queen Mother Hertha's following statement completely halts any attention I've been paying to the lesson for the rest of the period.

"Its scientific name is verecundiam, but it is generally known as the Shame Plant."

The Shame Plant. Where have I heard that? I have definitely heard that exact name before. Was it in the Queen's Doctor's story? Or was it in the story about Michelle that the Boggletrice Company told me? I wrack my brain to remember until the trumpets blast signaling time for High Noon Fare. The class reluctantly takes their Shame Plants and files through the wisteria; little moans and even shouts along the way.

There are a thousand things I'd rather do than go to High Noon Fare, but I go and pick at the meaty lump that is supposed to be meatloaf but more resembles a heap of dead animal. Two Einsreich, a boy and a girl, are staring at the floor right by our table. King Klauschwitz pats the boy on the shoulder as casually and comfortably as if it were his own son. Tritch Anguis is as snobby as ever, but I do notice he will not touch the terrible meat thing either. Elbows on the table, he laces his fingers, "How are your studies going, Maggie?"

"Fine," I reply dully.

"Fine *what?*" he snips.

I clench my teeth. "Fine...*King Tritch.*"

"That's better. High time we've enforced the rules with you." He says this in a way that I know he means many more rules than just Emily Castle's. Tritch couldn't care less about my studies except maybe the ones with Stiorri. He sips his Bubblegin.

"Why do we have to study the verecundiam?" I ask, hoping he will say something that jogs my memory.

"Why not?" he replies flatly.

I roll my eyes.

"The verecundiam is a rare breed that has many magical properties," says Klauschwitz. "An extraordinary plant worthy of royalty."

"Yeah, but the Hanging Gardens have plenty of plants that aren't so—so shameful."

"Your grant to speak has already expired, but if you must know, the verecundiam has been a staple at Emily for generations, and with the recent improvements, we need more of it than usual."

I say nothing. It's on the tip of my brain. *Think, Maggie, think.*

The rest of the day cannot go by fast enough. I do not listen to a thing in Michelle Academics except that all books are off-limits. Toadi drawls on and on about Emily's involvement in world trade. I doze in and out on the arm of the sofa until, thankfully, I happen to hear her say, "...verecundiam. Emily imported mass quantities of the plant for use in developing the castle we know today."

Ugh! Shame Plant, Shame Plant...

Michelle put it in something here. What was it? I am so angry with myself for not being able to remember.

My next class is Subjects with Queen Mother Erline, which I don't pay attention to either, and I end up embarrassed when she calls on me to recite the royal address she taught us.

"You're a Regina, Princess Maggie. This is disappointing," Queen Mother Erline scolds.

In Science, Queen Mother Felberta makes sure to whisper, "Strange times, Princess, strange times. I fear we mustn't speak much, you and I, but know I am with you in thought and deed."

"Thank you, Queen Mother. You are right that it is very strange times."

When the trumpets blast, signaling the night feast, I could not be happier, even if I do have to sit with the gloom crew until it's over. Happy about *what*, I'm not sure exactly. I think it's happiness that the wait to meet Clair Shelley is finally almost over, and I might find out *something* that will be helpful in this mess. That is, if Clair actually does ensure that I make it down to the dungeon.

But as I sit eating the junk meant for the verecundiams instead of the slop that is supposed to be dinner, I grow more and more anxious that the Anguises and Klauschwitz will never let me out of their sight. I usually walk with Thorn back to our dormitory. What will I tell her as to where I'm going? She will undoubtedly tell her father whatever I say.

As the time draws near the end of the feast, the Einsreich on the floor begin laughing hysterically their creepy and ominous laughter. When they do, all the flying carpets in the room drop, and many plates and goblets being flown to and from the balconies crash to the floor. The two Einsreich by us lift their pale, zombie heads and their red eyes squint as they burst out in jaunty laughter.

"What's this about, Klauschwitz?" exclaims Tritch, but Klauschwitz is already up looking them over.

Still laughing hysterically, the Einsreich girl by Tritch puts her hands over his eyes. He yells, trying to pry them off, but the young giant royal is much too strong for him. "Help, Klauschwitz! What are they doing?"

Thorn doesn't move or speak but only watches her father's peculiar predicament. Something tells me this isn't by chance. Without giving myself time to think, I get up. Thorn's eyes shift to me.

"Better be going, mate!" And with that, I'm off, running to the statue of Pippin.

Chapter 16
The Eyes in the Wall

I run as fast as I can to Ironsnout Hall, climb onto Pippin, and spin the pages of Pippin's Puzzle, which begin turning rapidly on their own. I bet this statue and the book are another thing Pippin dropped in Emily against Michelle's wishes, like Cervi Day. But again, this begs the question of why Pippin doesn't just come and take over the whole thing. The statue flips and I am on my back in the dungeon in a second. Without Magnus to illuminate my path, all is dark. I can't even see my hands. I step carefully down the descending walk to the dungeon floor with my hands out in front of me but stumble and roll downward until I hit something—a foot. I can see it. I look above me at an Einsreich girl's face, her red dead eyes staring vacantly yet dreadfully down at me. I open my mouth to scream—

"Princess!"

I look in the direction of the voice to see that the reason the room is no longer dark, and I can see this hideous face of the

Einsreich, is because Clair Shelley illuminates the whole room. She now has a ghostly glow when she looked somewhat normal in the dormitory. "Princess, come," she whispers.

I follow Clair into a cell. It is the one Wes and Jack were in when we were all being held here. I shudder remembering and hesitate to go in. Who is this girl, or ghost, after all? "Why are we going in there?" I ask suspiciously.

Clair indicates the Einsreich. "We've seen these things come to life from time to time down here. We thought this would be safest just in case."

"We?"

Just as I say the word, illuminated by Clair's glow, two eyes blink open in the cell's back wall. They are the eyes that McShanihan spoke to when he rescued me from the dungeon after I killed Louie and Julian. But now, a mouth also emerges beneath the eyes and speaks with a woman's voice. "It's alright, Princess Maggie. You can trust us."

For some reason, I do trust them and go into the cell with Clair Shelley and the face. Clair closes the gate, and she and I sit on the cold stone floor. The face lowers itself to our level.

"First things first. Maggie, Gemma, Gemma, Maggie."

I gasp. "Gemma? Queen Gemma the Extraordinary?"

Gemma laughs. "Not so extraordinary. Princess Maggie, you have proven far more extraordinary than I ever could have been."

"No way. You were an amazing queen. Everyone in Emily and Little Ipswich knows you and loves you. You did so much for the town. I loved reading about you in history and hearing about you from—" I stop myself before I say something stupid.

The mouth smiles but the eyes are melancholy. "I am glad that I was able to accomplish some important things, but now I know I should have focused on more important things than even those."

And then I do say a stupid thing. "Why did you give up and take your own life?" As soon as the words leave my lips, I wish I could grab them and send them back the other way. What's wrong with me?

The eyes widen in surprise but do not seem offended. "Oh yes. That is a terrible rumor. And I am sorry to say that it is all my fault that it began. When it came out about Michelle murdering the Snickerlings, I came here to the dungeon and wrote a very dramatic letter one night. And yes, I was in the darkest place I'd ever been. But I would never have killed myself. I loved my people too much and had every intention of fighting for them. I had already set a few of my most trusted Snickerlings to secretly build a passageway between Lazy Jug and the castle. I had begun a plan to make things right."

I am dumbfounded. This doesn't make any sense. I was told by the Queen's Doctor, the Boggletrice Company, *and* the ancestors that Gemma had taken her own life in the dungeon and that McShanihan had found her with a note. The story goes that even Michelle himself was surprised by it. What in the world is she saying?

"You'll understand in a minute," Clair Shelley says, apparently witnessing my mental gymnastics.

The face that is Gemma continues. "The reason everyone thinks that I took my own life is because just as I was nearing the end of my letter, I was approached by a man by the name of Cassian Anguis. I had seen him before in my dealings with the town. He was a rich man from a family of Victor's Spoil. He said nothing to me, but I could tell that he had murder on his mind because of the manic look in his eyes and the dagger in his hand. It was he who killed me that night and then carefully mimicked my handwriting as he finished the letter saying that I was going to commit suicide."

"Cassian Anguis," I mutter. "So the Anguises have had their own agenda the whole time?"

"Yes, Michelle was completely caught off guard by the incident because he was unaware that the Anguises, like him, had no intention of anyone ruling Emily Castle but themselves. King McShanihan was told by his crown that I had been killed and where I was. It is true that he found me and took my body away. It is buried in the Forest of the Silver Birch."

"Michelle the Deceiver deceived by his own henchmen," muses Clair.

"Wow. But why are you here in the wall, Queen Gemma? And what about you, Clair?" I ask.

Clair and the face that is Gemma look at one another to see who will tell. Clair finally says, "We aren't really ghosts. More like memories."

THE EYES IN THE WALL

"Yes, that is all we can think of because we aren't quite like ghosts. If we are ghosts, the same ghostly rules do not apply to the two of us individually. Princess Clair is almost wholly the appearance of her living self, and she is able to travel the castle freely. I am only a face in the wall of the dungeon and catacombs. Maybe we are ghosts, but whatever we are now, we are certainly something other than what we were before. We aren't even in the same place as our bodies—mine is in the Forest of the Silver Birch, and Clair's is in the Lux Sea."

"Strange. But why? Are there any other ghosts or memories besides you two?" I ask, questioning Pippin in my mind again. How could he let this happen?

"Just us as far as we know," says Clair.

"I wonder why. There have certainly been other people killed here, I'm sure." I don't mention that I killed two of them.

Clair shrugs. "Unfinished business maybe? To do our best to expose what this place is."

"And we haven't been able to make hardly any headway all these years until now, Maggie. And it's because of you," says Gemma.

I scratch my head. "You're kidding. I keep messing everything up."

The memories laugh. My cheeks go red.

"Oh, Princess, it may *feel* that way, but we assure you that you are the extraordinary one. Pippin made sure you made your way here, and you got Michelle exactly where he needed to be for

Pippin to slay his physical body. You killed Julian and Louie who were as wicked as the day is long."

Gemma saw that?

"You have boldly proclaimed the truth to the castle and continue to fight the fight even though many do not believe you. Maggie, you are a hero."

Now my cheeks are on fire. I am speechless. All I can manage is, "I have lost sight of Brumbletide. I cannot see the Digglewip." My voice cracks and my eyes start to water. I've never said it out loud before.

To my surprise, the eyes in the wall glimmer as the mouth smiles again. What could Gemma possibly be smiling about?

"Oh, dear girl, I am sure you are burying yourself alive over this. But do take heart, you have had sight once, you shall have it again if you only *remember*. I was queen—the "extraordinary" queen—and I never had sight at all until the very end."

What on earth is she talking about? "Gemma, whatever do you mean? You made it free to attend Emily Academy, and it was you who had the hospital built!"

"I loved the people of Emily. I wanted to do great things for them, the best things. But I never realized that the best thing was to bring them to Pippin and Brumbletide, the true king and the true kingdom. Sure, I made academy tuition free—now they had free access to the wicked castle fueled by murdered Snickerlings. Sure, I built a hospital—not only does it bear the name of the evilest man that ever lived, but his followers run it. I missed that to truly do good here, you must start with Pippin and his kingdom."

For about the thousandth time since coming to Emily, I'm speechless.

"I think you got her there, Gem," says Clair amused.

The face in the wall giggles. "Try to think about everything I've said, but let's get down to business, shall we?"

"I second that," says Clair. "Now that you know what happened to Gemma, let me tell you how I found myself in this state." She waves her hand through my arm.

"I'm *dying* to know." *Oh no. Really Maggie?* I could slap myself. Thankfully, Clair doesn't seem to mind and gets on with her story.

"As you probably gathered, my dormmate, Irene, and I were both Whitescales many years ago. We had heard rumors that royals were disappearing, but never really believed it until Irene's brother disappeared. She was a wreck and asked everyone where he went and if anyone had seen him. She went to the administration and told them about it. Certainly, they would be concerned that all these kids were going missing and call the Ipswich Police. But they didn't. They told her they were just as concerned as she was and were working on finding them, but no one was found, and Irene went missing a week later."

My skin prickles. I have seen a lot of terrible things at Emily by now, but there always seems to be something else that takes me by surprise.

"I was distraught. I didn't know what to do. I was afraid to go to the administration in case the same thing happened to me. I decided to confide in the girl who lived in the dormitory next to us, Felberta McHash. She was the Regina of Whitescale that year."

"Felberta...you don't mean Queen Mother Felberta?"

Clair Shelley sets a severe gaze. "I most certainly do."

"Wow! I never could have imagined Queen Mother Felberta being a student here."

"They all were students here," says Clair.

"Wild. Queen Mother Felberta had something happen to her recently. She was possessed by Michelle! He was in a crown that my dormmate, Thorn, gave her as a gift."

"We know, Princess. There is a reason she was able to be possessed. We'll get to that."

I must try hard to focus on what Clair is saying and not let my brain chase possible reasons why Michelle could possess Queen Mother Felberta.

"As Regina, Felberta went to the meetings for the heads of class. I thought for sure they would have been discussing the matter of the missing kids. But when I spoke to her, she had a strange look in her eyes. She was listening to me but seemed miles away at the same time. I will never forget what happened next as long as I am not living."

I brace myself.

"Felberta told me that she knew exactly where all of the students were. I was shocked. I did not feel a hint of relief. Why in the world would she know where they were and not say anything to anyone? She then seemed to focus; she was no longer a million miles away. She told me that she would show me where they were."

Oh no, this is that part in Dad's horror movies where the stupid victim goes precisely to the room that is obviously the place where they will die. But Clair doesn't seem stupid. What was she thinking?

"I wasn't about to go with her anywhere! She gave me the creeps."

Oh, good! Where is this story going then?

"But suddenly, Felberta got hungry. She said she was starving and asked if I wanted something to eat. I was thrown off. So strange. She got her satchel and took out two candy bars I'd never seen before. She said the Whitescale Rex and Regina got to participate in a first-time experiment of making the world's best chocolate. She was positively raving about how delicious it was and how fun it was to make. She asked me to try some, and I declined but she kept pushing, and because I wanted so badly to continue the discussion of the missing children, I took a bite." Clair pauses.

"And then what?" I ask in suspense.

"And this happened." She indicates her translucent body. "The chocolate killed me! And I still don't know what happened to the other royals. If the same thing happened to them, why am I the only one still hanging out in Emily Castle all these years later?"

"That's the most frustrating story ever!" I exclaim angrily.

"You're telling me!" pipes Clair angrily.

"Unbelievable! Felberta is wicked after all? I don't get it. She saw Pippin restore my friend Calysta to life after being turned to stone. She seemed to be good then. She seems good now!"

"Hang on a minute, she is good," says Clair. "She's being controlled."

"But how?"

"Through the years, I have been able to observe a lot. Not everything. But a lot. I still don't know where those kids went, and I don't know why I am still here, but I do know that Felberta can be completely controlled by Emily officials when given certain items."

"I keep hearing about the Emily officials. Who the heck are they anyway?"

It is Gemma who says, "The Clan of Anguis."

"Of course," I say.

"They stay hidden the best they can, Maggie. They do not want to ruin the façade. Felberta has no idea she is being used now and again for their purposes. That time with the crown wasn't the first. They did the same with the Rex of our house that year, Julian Sanborn."

"You don't mean the Julian that killed my dad?"

"That's the one. Julian and Felberta weren't just trying new experiments the rest of us weren't. They *were* experiments."

"So Julian was being controlled when he killed my dad?" I grab fistfuls of my hair and squeeze my eyes shut. "Did I kill an innocent man? But he wasn't innocent! He killed my dad!"

"Maggie, listen!" It's the face in the wall that is Gemma.

THE EYES IN THE WALL

"You did nothing wrong."

"You did absolutely nothing wrong, Maggie," adds Clair. "Julian was bad from the beginning. I watched as they controlled him several times, but he looked up to the Anguises and became loyal. They didn't have to control him after a while, and he killed your father fully aware of what he was doing."

My head starts to spin from the roller coaster of emotions. This is all so insane.

"Felberta, on the other hand, is good as gold and certainly needs to be controlled. There was something in that chocolate that killed me but *fueled* her somehow. She won't even be able to tell you how because she is still unaware of it to this day."

"Gosh," is all I can manage.

"We want to help you figure it out, Maggie," says Gemma. "We want to do what we can to expose the truth."

I breathe a deep, deep sigh. "Well, I appreciate that. But now, not only was I captured and brought here to Emily so I'm no help to the Chosen or the Boggletrice Company—" Gemma gasps. "Ah! Tell me about them all."

"Who?"

"The Chosen! I was awe-stricken seeing them rescue you all with their warmouths. The whole event was breathtaking. And who is this Boggle...Boggle..."

"Oh, yes. That's a long story about the Chosen. The Boggletrice Company is a group outside the castle fighting for Pippin and Brumbletide. Gus, the bartender of Lazy Jug, Martha, the baker—"

"Gus! Martha! Oh, Gus and Martha. My dear friends. I saw them here in the dungeon. The time was not right to reveal myself, but I kept watch over them. How on earth are they still alive and well all these years later?" Gemma's voice is over the moon.

I completely forgot that Gemma was friends with Gus and Martha when they were kids! "That's right, you know them! Gus told me, but I forgot. They are still alive because Pippin left them the Scepter of the Seven. It makes them age very slowly, and they held on like champions through our capture."

"Incredible! Oh, I must see them again. How wonderful. What wonderful news, indeed."

Gemma's excitement only makes me feel worse. I will surely fail, and now I have someone else to disappoint. "I do hope you get to see them again, but I am so awful at being a hero. Please do not get your hopes up."

"Maggie, as I said before, you have done extraordinary things already, you will do them again. Your problem is that you think it is *you* getting it all done."

"Well, who is it then?"

There is a pause as if Gemma is waiting for me to finally understand the obvious. Nothing hits me.

"Maggie, it's Pippin! You are his chosen one to do his work for a time such as this, but he will get done what he intends. You've got to believe that."

"Then where is he?!" I shout and then clap my hands over my mouth both out of fear of being heard and because I have blatantly disrespected Pippin to a woman who adores him.

Clair shakes her head. Gemma, if she had a head would probably be doing the same.

Finally, Gemma says quietly. "I was where you are too. Really, I was. Even if you can't believe it now, what you can believe, and you must, is that you will be able to believe it when all is said and done. Can you do that, Maggie?"

"I don't know. But I'll try."

"Yes, try," Gemma says, and the wall smiles.

"We're running out of time," says Clair. "You must get back. But know that we are both looking out for you. I'm watching up there, and Gemma will be down here. You are not alone."

"Thank you so much. That means the world. And what about Stiorri, is she safe? I've been meeting with her."

"Good as gold. Same with Carrington of Disposition. They don't know everything happening around here, but you can rest assured they are on your side. I've watched the Queen Mothers through the years, and while they never said anything aloud, I could tell they distrusted the administration. I was the one who gave Carrington the Digglewip. Gemma told me it was kept in a vault in Michelle Tower and how to open it. It hadn't been touched for decades, so likely no one would notice if it was gone. It was tricky getting it out of the vault, but with Jericho's help, I was able to get it with a little manipulation of the scenery like what you saw in Throne Room tonight." Clair lifts her chin proudly.

"Well done," I laugh, relaxing a little. Without meaning to,

I find myself thinking, *Thank you, Pippin.*

"Alright, let's get you back to your dormitory," says Clair.

"Princess, it was sheer joy to meet you," says Gemma. "My eyes are on you."

"You too, Queen Gemma. You really are extraordinary." If the wall could blush, I know it would be now.

But as Clair and I stand up to leave, another question occurs to me. "Clair, can everyone see you?"

"No, not everyone."

"Well, how can Thorn and I see you then?"

"Ah, that is a good question. I only figured out the answer after several years of being this way. The only people that can see me are the ones who have taken life."

Clair and I lock eyes as we both consider the same thing. Who, then, has Thorn killed?

Brynn Miller, age 12

Chapter 17
Useless, Stupid, Failure

The face melts back into the wall, and Clair Shelley puts an arm around me. "Let's get you back to your room. Come with me. I know a new way to Whitescale."

We go to the dungeon's hidden entrance, and at once, the wall opens to the secret staircase that McShanihan and I took the night I killed Julian and Louie—apparently the only reason I can see Clair Shelley. At the top of the stairs is a door that leads to the long corridor of many doors. Does Clair know about the Boggletrice Company Headquarters?

"How did you find this place?" I ask.

"Lots of time to explore these forty years. Followed McShanihan several times this way. Or who I think is McShanihan anyway, he looks different every time."

I gaze down the hall at the round red door at the end that leads into the Boggletrice Company. "Have you ever been in that one at the end? That red door there?" I ask.

"No. Gemma told the Snickerlings to make it as secret as possible after she learned the truth about Emily. It's only visible to those invited in. I can't go in anyway. I can't leave the castle. I've tried. It's like there's an invisible wall that I can't pass through."

"I'm sorry."

"Hey, it's alright. Keeps me searching for answers. Nothing else to do."

We enter a white door with a golden window that is fogged so you can't see through it. "I can't open it, but I'll see what's on the other side. Wait here." Clair goes through the wall. My hair stands on end watching her. In a second, she is back. "Coast is clear. I'll take you to your dormitory. As far as Thorn knows, I'm a real live student, and we are just together as friends."

"Alright."

I open the white door. Across the hall is the statue of Soleil holding a set of scales. When we go to the dormitory, our plan is foiled. Thorn is in the room—but so are Tritch and Klauschwitz.

"Maggie, we do not tolerate rebellion at this academy. Who are you?" His black eyes have shifted to Clair. He sees her.

Clair looks worried. Can all three see her? "I-I live in the dormitory next door."

I see that both Tritch and Klauschwitz have their eyes fixed on Clair. They both see her. That means they too have killed. Of course they have.

"Well, get back to it," pipes Tritch. "Being out of your

USELESS, STUPID, FAILURE

dormitory after curfew is an offense punishable by dungeon. This is your warning. Next time, you will be severely punished."

"Yes, Your Majesty." Clair curtsies and hurries out of the room.

"Where were you?" Tritch asks me with slitted eyes.

"Nowhere."

"Stop the nonsense. You will lose your life," Tritch whispers harshly. "Tell us what you were doing. Were the ancestors with you?"

"No."

"What were you doing? Final chance."

"Before what? I wasn't doing anything. I went for a walk with a friend."

Tritch holds a dead stare at me. His long face sags at the mouth. I am uneasy, but I stare right back. Is it possible that I hate him *more* than Michelle?

"You will stay with me."

"Father, I'll watch her," says Thorn.

"You will, will you? Because you've been doing such a superb job of it so far?"

Tritch grabs my arm. "She's staying with me. Klauschwitz, bring the verecundiam and some of her things."

"But she will see, Anguis."

"So what? She won't be around much longer for it to matter." Tritch yanks and drags me by the arm to and through the Throne Room to his chambers. These are Lenore's former chambers, and they were mine for a very short time. But when we enter, the room looks much different than it used to. The first time I was in this room was when I was desperately searching for the twin's onyxes. I remember coming in here and being so disheartened when I saw hundreds of crowns lining the walls, each with its own shelf. I would have to search every single one for the stones that turned out not to be in any of them. Then I was in here a few times—only a few—as Head of Emily Castle. But they still looked more or less the same as when they were Lenore's chambers. But today, you would never guess that this is the same room. On every shelf that once held a crown now sits a silvery, leafy verecundiam. All of them set together is a wall of sinister leaves. When we burst into the room, hundreds of Shame Plants scream, "You've lost sight of the kingdom!"

Tritch throws me on the floor. "You will stay here for the remainder of your days."

Shortly after, Klauschwitz walks in with my verecundiam, a bag of gowns, and two Einsreich boys who position themselves on either side of me. "They have been ordered to attack if you go near the door. But it will be locked anyway."

"I will retrieve you in the morning and take you to your class," Tritch explains as if he is speaking to scum on his shoe. With that, he and Klauschwitz leave, and the Einsriech take their place in the room's corners. The door is then shut and locked from the outside.

"Now what?" I toss myself on the giant canopy bed. The room is dark. The torchless flames flicker sporadically—more

USELESS, STUPID, FAILURE

Einsreich magic. In the flickering light, the Einsreich's creepy, red eyes are more chilling than usual.

And then the Shame Plants press in. They all chant in wicked unison, "You've lost sight! You'll never get it back!"

"Useless! You're useless. You know it too!"

"Stupid girl. Who ever thought you could do anything?"

"Look at you. Failure. Such an utter failure."

"Useless!"

"Stupid!"

"Failure."

"They had the wrong one from the start!"

I cover my head with the pillow, but it's no use; the hissing and screeching of hundreds of verecundiams cannot be muffled. My throat tightens because the worst part of it is that they are right. I am useless and stupid and a failure. I have been this whole time. I've known it this whole time and there is no way the Chosen and the Boggletrice Company haven't known it this whole time as well. Somewhere, there is another Daughter of Eve floating around, probably still at Little Ipswich High School. She probably eats dinner with her two parents who help her with her homework afterward, and they are all getting excited about the holiday they will be taking in the spring. Maybe it's my cousin, Lea, in the States.

I'm not tired at all. How am I supposed to sleep with these things carrying on all night?

"Shut up!" I yell, but of course, it changes nothing. The

hissing only seems to get worse. "Shut uuuuuuuuup!" I yell again. It's more of a release than anything.

As soon as my lips close from yelling there is a rustling of the Shame Plant leaves, and light bursts forth as two white antlers poke through them.

I gasp. "Pippin! Pippin, thank God!"

The White Stag emerges from the leaves and saunters slowly through the room, looking straight ahead. The Einsreich do not budge. Pippin doesn't seem to notice them, but he doesn't seem to notice me either.

"Pippin! I'm right here! So glad you came. Please, get me out of here!"

But the Stag keeps walking past the bed all the way to the other wall and then right *through* it. He's gone.

I stare at the wall in disbelief. I can't take it. What in the world is Pippin doing? Where is he going? Why won't he help me? "What is wrong with you? Can't you see I'm right here and need help?" I'm yelling. "Why don't you *do something* about all of this? They're going to kill me, you know! Did you hear me? They are going to *kill* me!"

Nothing.

I can't hold back any longer. "AAAAAAAAAAAAHHHHH!"

The door flies open. Tritch Anguis's black eyes are fiery and, with the flickering light, appear utterly wicked. "Quiet, or I'll kill you tonight. Do not test me, girl." He slams the door and locks it again.

I throw myself backward, bury my face in a pillow, and

scream until my throat scratches. Exhausted and teary, I lay lifeless and defeated.

"Useless!"

"Stupid!"

"Failure!"

But a voice—I know the voice—quiet yet somehow deep and resounding fills the room so much the leaves of the Shame Plants shake.

"Remember, Maggie. Remember your letter. Remember."

"Remember what?" I say into the air quietly.

But, of course, there is no response.

Chapter 18
The Treehouse Deer

It's only been minutes, but it feels like hours. I've been lying here crying and hopeless, believing more and more the words of the Shame Plants.

There is a rustling in the leaves on the wall. I sit up. "Pippin?" But there is nothing. I return to my teary hopelessness. A few minutes later, I hear a different sound, a crunching noise. It is loud and crisp and constant. I look around, straining my eyes to see between the leaves of the Shame Plants, but there is still nothing as far as I can tell. I look over the Einsreich boys, which I hate because they're so creepy. They are both still as stone. Do they even breathe?

The crunching grows louder and closer, and now there is smacking as well.

"Is anyone there?" I whisper, trembling.

The crunching stops momentarily, and two gleaming, scaly

wings pop into view at the side of the bed, and a happy, panting, slobbering dragon jumps into my lap, licking my face profusely.

"Zelda, girl! You have no idea how glad I am to see you!" I hug Zelda's scaly neck. "I thought you were in Mozambique with Soleil."

The wiggly white dragon wriggles and wags in excitement.

"What in the world was all that racket you were making?"

Zelda jumps down, sticks her head under the bed, and returns with a mouthful of verecundiam leaves. I hang over the edge and look under to see probably another hundred plants stuffed under the bed as well. "Blimey, what are they doing with all of these?"

Zelda gets herself one more mouthful and then snuggles up next to me. My heart is about to burst with the joy of the dragon being here. Pippin must have brought her. But why doesn't he do anything else?

I stroke Zelda's lumpy back as she finishes up her midnight snack. To my delight, I realize I can no longer hear the Shame Plant's shrieks now that she is beside me. With the quiet, I am finally able to think. Only one thing comes to mind. It is a giant black billboard in my brain with one word on it in white capital letters.

REMEMBER.

Then a voice sounding like Eve's says it. "Remember."

The white word in all capitals is plastered behind my eyelids when I close them. Now, another woman's voice, much like Eve's but lighter, speaks. I'm almost sure it's Queen Mother

Stiorri. "Remember." She says the word urgently like I need to remember soon or there will be consequences. Frustration and panic begin stirring inside me again.

The word pulsates in my brain in tandem with my heartbeat. "Remember...remember...remember...remember..."

And now a man's voice. It is not Pippin's. It is not George's or Justice's. It is a man's voice I know very well and didn't get to hear nearly enough. "Remember, Mags," says Dad.

"Dad," I croak as my eyes fill with tears. "Do you believe any of it? Where are you? Remember what?" Tears stream my face.

There is no response. When I close my eyes again the big white REMEMBER is gone. Now I see a badger wearing a soft sweater and glasses. The Messenger happily walks through my mind seemingly unaware he is there. He holds a sign that rests on his shoulder. Of course, it reads, *Remember*.

The frustration and panic have built up to the point that I want to scream, but Zelda shifts to a more comfortable position and stretches herself along my side. When she does, suddenly screaming doesn't seem like such a good idea. She closes her eyes, and I feel her warm, comforting breath on my cheek. I remember Soleil saying Zelda doesn't even know she can breathe fire. The dragon's peaceful sleep calms me, and I ponder "remember" without anger. Finally, I decide that I will try to remember everything—thirteen years of everything.

I don't remember much before our late-night trips to Nan's Pancakes. Those are by far my favorite memories. Not just with

Dad, those are my best memories *ever*. I strain my mind, but I have almost nothing with my mother. Why? When did she decide she didn't like us or want us? It's like there is a black wall when it comes to Mum. I haven't been around many other mothers for any length of time, and I'm wise enough to know the TV mums are not how mums really are. But my whole life, I had this feeling that the way my mum was wasn't the way mums are supposed to be toward their children. The other kids' mums would be at school holiday parties and things, but not mine. And just the way those mums *were* with their kids, I could tell it was real. They *liked* their kids. And come to think of it, Grandma was a mum too! She was Dad's mum. And she was absolutely wonderful. What happened to my mother? As much as I don't want to, I try to remember good times with Mum. Strangely, the best time I ever had with her was at Emily during the Cervi Day feast. It was the one and only time we had been together acting like an actual family. She, Wes, and I even talked and laughed as she told us about Bubblegin and—

My eyes pop open. I sit up. Zelda's head pops up, alert. How has it never occurred to me before? I remember the night I asked Mum to take us to Batch after seeing the scary movie. I remember her saying she grew up attending Emily! But she didn't attend Emily Academy. How did she meet Dad? If she was dating Dad and Emily officials knew he was a Son of Eve, maybe they did something to her. Maybe Emily had a hand in why Mum is the way she is. Maybe they gave her something like whatever was in the Snowdrop Frost dessert that made everyone forget the ancestors were ever at the castle. That must be it. For the first time in my life, I want to go see my mother. But I can't. I wonder if anyone here knows her.

Feeling I've hit a dead end, I lay back down and close my eyes again. Zelda gets up and turns in circles several times before snuggling up and resting her head on my belly.

The badger is back. He stands in my mind with the sign. *Remember.*

I think of Wes. I remember when he was born. Dad had lifted me up to look through the hospital window at Mum holding the new bundle that was Wes. I didn't like him very much back then, but he's been a good little brother for the most part. I remember him taking his first steps and saying his first word. It was "moon." He loved space even as a baby. I remember the two of us playing in the yard all those times, and I remember the two of us striking up the idea of the treehouse—the treehouse I now know is in the Forest of the Silver Birch. I remember how determined we were. It felt like building the treehouse was our job for the summer, and every day we had to show up to work. We'd get up, get ourselves a juice and a toaster pastry, and discuss where to find the materials we needed that day. Then we'd set out on our mission to acquire them, and once we had, it was off to the forest to build.

Now that I am thinking back, there was something strange that happened one day when we arrived at the construction site. We had already built most of the house, and this day, we were carrying Dad's ladder that we were only going to borrow until we built one of our own. But Dad's ladder ended up being the ladder that we used forever. As we approached the wall of fir trees, we heard rustling. Wes and I stopped to listen. I could tell Wes was a little nervous. I was too. We were in the middle of the woods; it could be a bear or something! What if it had rabies?

After a long hesitation, I laid down my end of the ladder and told Wes I was going to check it out. Slowly, carefully, and quietly, I peeked through the trees.

It was a deer. He was standing right there in the middle of our treehouse site. I was delighted to see him. We never saw deer. He was beautiful. I called Wes quietly to come see. He set the ladder down and quietly came to stand by me to get a look. He gasped. The deer looked right at us. We didn't know what to do. I had never heard of a vicious deer, but the tall and sharp-looking antlers on this one were unnerving. What if he charged at us? We waited and waited, but the deer seemed to be going nowhere soon.

I told Wes to stay behind the tree and I would walk toward it. Surely it would run away as soon as I rustled the branches. If it ran at us, we would speed away immediately.

I took a deep breath and stepped through the trees. The deer looked at me but didn't budge. I swear he even seemed glad to see me! His feet did a little dance like he had been wondering when we would finally come out and now we had. The deer and I looked at each other for a little while. I remember its green eyes, but he was brown not white, so it couldn't have been Pippin. I moved around some boards and things to show the deer I was planning on working in that area. He continued to follow me with his eyes but didn't move. After a while, I sensed that this deer would not harm us, so I went and got Wes and the two of us brought the ladder through the trees. When we returned, the deer had now knelt on all fours like he was settling in to watch us work. He seemed very interested in what we were doing. Of course, Wes had to try to pet him. I hadn't realized it until he was already over at the deer stroking its back. I opened my mouth to yell at him, but the deer seemed perfectly alright with Wes petting him, so I decided to give it a try myself. And that is when it happened.

The second I touched the deer, suddenly, I was on a mountaintop with him. The deer was standing tall looking out over the Lux Sea at Emily. It lasted only a second, and then we were in the woods again.

I'd forgotten all about that until now. Some sort of strange daydream. Very strange considering there is no mountain anywhere close to Little Ipswich.

And the deer, it couldn't have been Pippin, right?

Chapter 19
Another Dragon

What happened next, no one, and I do mean absolutely no one on earth, saw coming. Until now, this story has been about Emily and its evil, as well as Brumbletide and Pippin. But on this cold February morning, the story expanded. Everyone woke up to the world in utter chaos. Not just Emily or Little Ipswich—*everywhere*. All of England was in a panic because children everywhere had been taken from their homes in the night.

Thorn came into Tritch's chambers this morning. Zelda hid immediately, but I'm pretty sure Thorn saw her. She told me that it was all over the news: thousands of children missing. Electronics of any kind are not allowed in Emily, but apparently, Tritch has made an exception for himself. Thorn said news reporters had even crowded onto the ferry to try to interview her about it since she is Head of Castle.

"The kids taken are all between the ages of seven and

seventeen, Maggie. The ages kids attend Emily Academy."

"What do you think it means, Thorn? It can't be your dad Klauschwitz, can it? Blimey, it's all of England! They couldn't possibly—could they?"

For the first time, I see Thorn visibly upset. She holds her stomach and her voice is panicked. "I-I don't know. But I'm afraid they might have figured out a way."

Our eyes meet for the first time in weeks. Her beady black eyes somehow appear soft and afraid.

"Will you do anything?" I ask.

Thorn is now hugging herself. She is rarely anxious. Is she being truthful?

"I don't know what I can do, Maggie. This is so much bigger than me."

Under the bed, Zelda burps. Thorn raises a brow but says nothing. Maybe she is being truthful.

"I've got to go, but I will try to come by and keep you informed."

"Alright, stay safe, Thorn."

"You too, Maggie."

I roll my eyes. *Really?*

Thorn exits the chambers and Zelda pops from under the bed with a mouthful of verecundiam.

"Please, help yourself. Eat as much as you want."

The dragon cuddles next to me and munches happily. Not long after Thorn's exit, without any warning footsteps or anything, Tritch comes in slamming the door behind him. Completely caught off guard, Zelda is in plain sight. Tritch looks at us blankly at first as if he doesn't really know what he's seeing, but then his lips part into a deep grin. "Is this—could this be—a warmouth?"

He steps cautiously, yet gleefully, to Zelda as if he's happened upon a treasure chest.

"Stay away from her! She's dangerous!" I lie.

Zelda wags her tail and pants happily at Tritch. *What the? What is she doing?*

"Oh, I can see she's vicious," says Tritch dotingly. He slowly stretches his long fingers to her head and gives her a soft pet. Zelda closes her eyes and nestles against his hand blissfully.

This is horrible.

I watch in complete disbelief of the dragon's lack of any intuition toward evil. She can't possibly be this stupid, can she?

I open my mouth to yell, "Zelda, no!" but before I get a single word out, Zelda opens her eyes—they blaze with fire. I gasp.

She immediately spreads her wings. Her wingspan is far wider than one would ever guess, almost as if they have grown in this very moment. She screeches a scream that could shatter glass. Her razor-sharp teeth shine in the flickering light. The lumpy dragon is now gone and what remains is something terrible and extremely vicious.

Tritch recoils. Stunned, he doesn't scream. He is whiter than white. A stream of fire blazes from Zelda's nostrils, and in the next moment, Tritch's robes have gone ablaze. Now he screams and falls to the floor trying to roll the fire out. There is another screech and breath of fire, and the chamber door is gone.

Zelda snatches my gown in her strong jaws. I think this might be a rescue, but I am utterly terrified. My bones tremble as I hang from the dragon, totally vulnerable. She could do anything she wants to me; I'm completely at her mercy. Zelda flies us out of the chambers, into the Throne Room, and to the upper windows.

She throws me out the window.

I scream as I fall to my death. The cold air is an icy blast preparing me for burial at sea. I squeeze my eyes shut, preparing for impact. Freezing tears from wind and terror leave my eyes.

Another screech comes from above, and I soon land on the scaly back of terrible Zelda. I cling for dear life to her neck. Looking back at the castle, I see a large hole at the top of the Throne Room. It was a rescue. Zelda—brilliant, fantastic, dangerous Zelda—has rescued me!

"The Snickerlings just finished repairing the hole Pippin left," I laugh. "Thank you, girl. Oh, thank you for saving me!"

We fly through the night. What a moment. Of all the times I've crossed the Lux Sea, this is by far the best, even trumping last time when the ancestors and their Brumbletide warmouths rescued us from the dungeon. That time, Calysta and Atticus were on the verge of death, something I never want to experience again in my life. I kiss Zelda—ferocious Zelda—out of sheer relief.

"Ernie!" I exclaim. "Zelda, we've left Ernie!"

But Zelda only keeps flying toward the town. There is no way we'd be able to go back and get him. *Please, please, let him stay safe.*

ANOTHER DRAGON

We fly swiftly and quietly over the ferry that I see has two Einsreich standing guard on the deck. We even keep flying right over Downtown Ipswich. Are we not going to the headquarters? We fly over the Ipswich bridge and over the forest. When we finally begin to descend, I know where Zelda is taking me. She is taking me to the Little Ipswich Library. We descend and land right at the double doors with pig's snout knockers. I step off and kiss Zelda's forehead. As I do, she shrinks before my eyes into the jolly little thing I know. She rolls on her back panting madly, spent from the rescue. I kneel and rub her belly. "So you can breathe fire, after all, you wonderful dragon you."

Zelda whimpers and licks my arm.

"Alright, let's see if anyone's home." I get up and knock on the door. Zelda and I wait, still as stone, to see a light come on or hear footsteps.

"Maggie!"

We look overhead. Out of a window, two heads poke out. Miss Squaffletree and Calysta!

"Calysta! Miss Squaffletree!"

"We'll be right down, Miss Maggie. Hold tight!"

In seconds, the doors open, and Calysta bursts out and wraps me in a hug. I squeeze her tight. What an incredible surprise this night has turned out to be.

Miss Squaffletree wears a long nightgown, and her hair is down. She holds a lantern and motions us inside. "Come in, come in. Ah, who is this?" Zelda has sat on her feet, wanting rubs.

"That's Zelda, Soleil's warmouth. She rescued me from Emily."

"Wonderful! Where's Ernie?" Miss Squaffletree looks past me out the door.

"He's still there," I say sadly. "I guess Zelda couldn't save us both at the same time."

Miss Squaffletree looks at the lumpy little dragon on her feet. "Well of course she couldn't."

"She was…different…when she saved me."

"Come. I'll make some tea."

We all follow Miss Squaffletree into room eighteen. Once inside, she pushes on one of the bookshelves and turns it completely around. A full kitchen appears.

"Wow!" I exclaim.

"You have no idea, Maggie. I've been staying here since we all got separated that day. There are rooms upon rooms upon rooms!" Calysta tells me.

"So you've been here? Where is everyone else?"

"We will discuss everything here soon, but let's get tea first." Miss Squaffletree puts the kettle on and soon the three of us have piping cups of tea. Miss Squaffletree's is black. Calysta and I both add cream and sugar.

I close my eyes, breathing in the floral scent. "Oh, this is divine. Especially after the Einsreich tea at Emily." I tell them both about how the Einsreich magic is being used now instead of the Snickerling's and how the castle is even starting to sink because of it.

ANOTHER DRAGON

"They're doing themselves in," says Calysta.

"But doing a lot of damage to everything and everyone along the way," adds Miss Squaffletree.

"So how did you end up here, Calysta?"

"When the Einsreich were after us, and we all went different ways, I just ran as fast as I could. I had to swim the Lux canal because there were Einsreich on the bridge. I've never been so tired in my life, but I made it across and ran here after."

"Gosh! Any idea where the others are?"

Calysta shakes her head sadly.

"I hope everyone is safe."

Calysta is thoughtful. "If I had to guess, I would say that Wes got back to the headquarters. I saw him running that way. I think Atticus went with Soleil. I saw them close to one another."

"But you don't think they made it back to the headquarters as well?"

"Of course I don't know for sure, but somehow, I can't imagine them doing anything other than searching for the Golden Blood Warmouth."

"You think?" I ask skeptically.

"I think." Calysta sips her tea.

"Hmm," Miss Squaffletree ponders our conversation with her elbows on the table and cup in her fingers. Her eyes gaze into the distance. "What about those places Queen Soleil was saying she needed to go to?"

"I don't know, but I would be shocked if she didn't take

Atticus to find the Golden Blood Warmouth. Like her lucky nest said," Calysta says in much more confidence than I think necessary.

"Well, I hope so. What do we do in the meantime?" I ask, trying to switch the conversation to something constructive.

"That's what we've been trying to figure out. The town is flooded with Einsreich."

"How in the world did you get Ernie to Emily, Miss S.?"

"He showed up here. The Boggletrice Company sent him."

"No one knows Ernie is part of us," Calysta says, smiling.

"Correct. Ernie came to me and said that the Company had sent him and that he was supposed get into Emily somehow. I know that Ernie told them to send him here because he would always come here as a boy, and we had gotten to know each other over stories. What he didn't know, nor did any of the Boggletrice Company know, is that I have a long history with Emily, though they, Emily, do not know it. No one else would understand because no one knows the story. But you do, Maggie." Miss Squaffletree gives a knowing smile to me—who doesn't know.

"Which story?" I ask, feeling suddenly awkward.

Miss Squaffletree sips her tea. The lantern casts a soft glow on her gingerbread eyes. "Long ago, before the Squaffletrees ever thought to set up shop in Little Ipswich, this library was something very different. Any idea what it was?"

"No clue," I say, hanging on every word.

"This castle was a place where grand parties were thrown. Only the elite of the town were allowed. They would come and feast, and flash their money, and dance at royal balls." Miss Squaffletree pauses to see if any lightbulb has turned on over our heads. Calysta and I exchange shrugs.

Amused, Miss Squaffletree continues. "This library was the none other than Dragon's castle."

"What?" Calysta and I say in unison.

The story the ancestors told me slowly starts dripping into memory. "Are we talking about the same dragon? The only dragon I know that had a castle was the one that taught Michelle everything he knew."

"That's the one," Miss Squaffletree beams.

The cozy kitchen of the glorious library I've visited so many times now seems chilling. "That's repulsive!"

"It certainly was, yes. The Dragon was a terrible and tragic ruler. That is until Pippin did away with him! Once the Dragon was gone, this palace was vacant. And several years later, my family followed the words told to them by a wise wizard-looking man. You know him as King Mortimer—"

"King McShanihan!" exclaims Calysta gleefully.

"Indeed. My family arrived at a dark, broken-down building that everyone had sworn off as something that could never be restored. But somehow, my great great great grandparents knew it could be made into something completely new. And as the story goes, it could." The lantern glows romantically on Miss Squaffletree's gingerbread eyes that now glisten with pride and tears of joy.

"How wonderful," Calysta says joyfully.

"And I truly believe Pippin is doing the same thing with Emily," Miss Squaffletree adds.

"Oh, I hope so," says Calysta, falling back in her chair with the weight of the idea.

I sit, saying nothing, trying my best not to be skeptical. I was finally starting to think that I might be able to see the Digglewip if I looked at it. I can at least *try* to be optimistic that Emily could become something else—something not completely wicked. "That would be lovely," I finally add.

Brynn Miller, age 12

Chapter 20
The Golden Blood Warmouth

That night, Miss Squaffletree lent Calysta and me two of her nightgowns. She slept in the chaise lounge while Calysta and I took her bed. Zelda, unwilling to sleep alone, curled up at our feet, making for a pretty crowded arrangement, but I wouldn't have had it any other way.

I woke up to Miss S. brewing coffee. She is already dressed and looking the way I am used to seeing her. I sit up, trying not to wake Calysta, but she stirs and tries unsuccessfully to roll over with the snoring Zelda pinning her legs down. I hang my legs over the edge of the bed and rub my eyes. Miss S. notices I'm up.

"Go back to sleep, darling. You need to rest. I have to open the library, but I'll be in to check on you two. Stay in here. I don't think it's wise to make it known you are staying with me."

"Thanks, Miss S."

Calysta stirs again but still doesn't wake up. Miss

Squaffletree pours herself a mug of coffee and quietly exits room eighteen. She gives me a wink before softly closing the door.

I try to go back to sleep, but my eyes do not want to stay shut. Finally, I get up and pour myself a cup of coffee. I sit in the armchair and stare at Calysta hoping she'll feel it somehow and wake up. But she doesn't move.

I sip my coffee and am glad when Zelda finally gets up and comes to lie at my feet. "Glad you're awake, girl," I say, rubbing her head.

What now? I'm relieved to be out of Emily, but what will we do? I can't get back to Lazy Jug because of the risk of being caught again by the Einsreich or worse, Tritch. What are they all doing? Are Atticus and Soleil really off looking for the Golden Blood Warmouth? Are they in danger? And now there is the massive issue that children are disappearing from homes everywhere. Thank God Wes is with the Boggletrice Company. If he really is with them, that is.

I am startled by a knock on the door. Miss Squaffletree is already back followed by two filthy and stinky people. Zelda goes insane. She flies like lightning to the two grubby people and licks their nasty faces!

Once I can get a good look at them, I gasp and run to Soleil and Atticus, throwing my arms around them, uncaring if the dirt gets all over me. Zelda whimpers at finally seeing her mistress again and licks Soleil's hair profusely.

"I missed you, girl!" Soleil tells Zelda, holding her scaly head and kissing her snout.

"She saved me from Emily, Soleil!" I tell her. "She transformed into a dragon that wasn't at all like her. You wouldn't believe it. She breathed fire and everything!"

Soleil grins ear to ear. "How I wish I could have seen it! But I think I will get my chance."

Calysta pops up. She stares at all of us, groggily trying to make sense of the scene, and beams when she finally does. "Queen Soleil! Atticus!" She runs over and squeezes them both. Calysta and I now have dirty nightgowns. "Are you two alright? Did you find the Golden Blood Warmouth?"

Atticus is taken aback. "What? How did you know?"

Calysta shrugs.

"Princess Calysta, you are quite keen. None of you are going to believe this. I am still in disbelief myself," Soleil tells us excitedly. "I know where the Golden Blood Warmouth is!"

"Where?" we all say in unison.

Miss Squaffletree sits on the edge of the armchair. "Oh, stags, the patrons can take care of themselves for a few minutes. I've got to hear this. Tea anyone? I've got coffee too." She indicates the kitchen.

"Have you got anything to eat? I'm starving," says Atticus.

"I sure do, Master Atticus. Coming right up. Follow me into the kitchen. I don't want to miss a thing!"

In no time, there is tea and sandwiches on the table, and we're all seated with refreshments in hand waiting for Soleil's news. Finally, after a large bite of a sandwich and a sip of tea, Soleil begins. "When we were all so rudely separated, I was blessed to find Prince Atticus had followed me to a wilderness behind the town."

I've never heard the field between Downtown Ipswich and Dragon Street described quite that way.

"Once we were clear of the Einsreich we hid in some shrubs and sat wondering what to do. After much deliberation, I told Prince Atticus that we should go ahead and be off to find the items needed to make the elixir that I thought might turn the Einsreich back into real children."

Atticus, with a mouthful of sandwich, raises his hand. "I would just like to say that there wasn't much deliberation at all. Like almost zero deliberation."

Soleil continues seamlessly. "But for some strange reason, I could not get the Golden Blood Warmouth out of my mind. What was it? Was it, in fact, real and not only a legend after all? So, I thought and thought and finally couldn't take it anymore. I told Prince Atticus that I had to figure out what the Golden Blood Warmouth was all about."

"I feel like the way she tells the story makes it seem like there was a lot more time spent thinking it over than there was," Atticus says, reaching for another sandwich.

"And then, Prince Atticus had the most brilliant idea to try the treehouse in the wood because King McShanihan might be there like he was before!"

"Yeah, that was pretty brilliant," Atticus agrees proudly.

"So off we went. Prince Atticus took me straight there, and

low and behold, King McShanihan was there."

Of course he was! What's with him and my treehouse?

"We asked him immediately about the Golden Blood Warmouth. He admitted he didn't know much but took off his glorious crown and asked it to tell us the legend again. The legend goes that during the Battle of Crescent and Fall—"

"Excuse me!" It's Calysta.

Soleil looks as though ice has been dropped on her head. "Yes, Princess?"

"Which one is the Battle of Crescent and Fall? I've only heard of the Battle of Ipswich. I swear I hear that title used for different battles. Or am I just confused?"

"I can answer that," says Miss Squaffletree. "The Battle of Ipswich is the proper name for the largely unknown battle—that wasn't really a battle at all, mind you—between Pippin and the Dragon. The reason it is called The Battle of Ipswich is because after that, Pippin changed the name of the town from Crescent and Fall to Little Ipswich, and that has been the name ever since. But you are right that people *do* call the Battle of Crescent and Fall, the great battle fought between Michelle and the Chosen, the Battle of Little Ipswich. This is because battles are usually named after the place they are fought, and since only a few people know there even was a battle between the Dragon and Pippin, they call the Battle of Crescent and Fall the Battle of Ipswich, unknowing there is already one by the same name. Although, mind you again, almost no one knows that it was, in fact, Michelle that the Battle of Crescent and Fall, known by most as the Battle of Ipswich, was fought against, but only some mysterious unnamed 'dark one'."

We all listen with baffled looks when the only one confused before was Calysta.

"I think what she's trying to say is that long story short, Michelle fought the Chosen in the Battle of Crescent and Fall, and Pippin killed the Dragon in the Battle of Ipswich."

"Yes, Master Atticus, that pretty much sums it up."

"Ok, thank you. Please continue, Queen Soleil," says Calysta.

"The legend of the Golden Blood Warmouth goes that during the Battle of Crescent and Fall, amongst the slain lay a warmouth, dead, never to fly again. But when Pippin was killed on that fateful day and his blood flooded the field, that warmouth was covered in the blood of Pippin—and it brought it back to life! When it was resurrected, it was different than before. Better. Changed."

"Wow! So which one is it?" I ask anxiously. "Was it one of the warmouths that rescued us from the dungeon that night?"

"It's Zelda!" exclaims Atticus.

"Zelda?" the rest of us reply, and everyone shifts to the little lumpy dragon who sits proudly by our table wiggling her tail.

"It's Zelda! I can't believe I've missed it all these years. After the battle, all of us were so heartbroken because we had lost our loved ones to Michelle. And not that I had it worse by any means, but realizing your brother is a wicked deceiver that led everyone astray made for a bad day. Anyway, I never had even the slightest notion that Zelda had come to the battle. I wasn't paying attention and thought surely she had stayed in Brumbletide. But when we returned to the castle, all the warmouths were there except Zelda. I couldn't find her anywhere. I had started to worry until she finally showed up later that night. She looked the same as far as I could tell, but there was something different about her. I couldn't put my finger on it; I just thought perhaps she was flustered with everything that had gone on. But over the years, she would disappear here and there and come back filthy or flustered like she'd been through the trenches. Listening to the legend again, it finally made sense. It was Zelda who had lost her life and was resurrected that day," Soleil's voice cracks at this.

My heart sinks thinking of the sweet, friendly dragon dead on the battlefield. But she was really something when she rescued me last night. I recount to Atticus and Soleil how she grew into a vicious dragon with fire in her eyes, blew fire at Tritch Anguis, and burst out of the Throne Room ceiling like Pippin did when he killed Michelle.

Soleil kneels by her dragon. "Good girl, good girl." Zelda rolls on her back to receive belly rubs. Soleil happily obliges.

"So what now? How will Zelda help us with all the kids that have disappeared around the country?"

"What do you mean, Princess Maggie?"

"It's all over the news. Thousands of children are gone from their homes all over England. Thorn told me back at Emily. She was really anxious, and I got the feeling she thinks her dad is behind it."

"How utterly tragic! We must leave at once," exclaims Soleil.

"And do what?" I ask.

"I'm not sure exactly, but I do know how we can start." Soleil holds up a large syringe.

"What's that for?" asks Calysta, holding her arm as if to protect it from the long needle before her.

Soleil goes to Zelda who senses danger and growls.

"Oh, come now, girl. It won't hurt too badly. And I promise I'll be quick."

Zelda turns her head away, whimpering, but allows Soleil to draw blood from her back leg. To all of our surprise, Zelda's blood is actually golden!

"It's beautiful!" exclaims Calysta.

"Astonishing!" breathes Miss Squaffletree.

"Blimey," mutters Atticus who hates needles.

Once the syringe is full, Soleil squirts it into a dark glass bottle from her bag. She then puts a small bandage on Zelda's leg and kisses her snout. "Thank you, my love."

Zelda pants happily.

"It is my thought that there are magical, restorative properties in Zelda's blood that may reverse what has been done to the Einsreich."

"Are you sure? How do you know?" I ask.

"I am not sure, Princess, nor do I know, but the Einsreich were infused with warmouth blood. The lucky nest then instructed me to find the Golden Blood Warmouth. So, we have warmouth blood being used for evil in the Einsreich, and it would make sense that the Golden Blood Warmouth, resurrected into something extraordinary by Pippin's blood, might have blood that could be used for good."

"But what do we do with it? Have them drink it?" asks Atticus with a wince.

"Well, we could, but I don't think we'll have much luck with those iron jaws of theirs. Plus, to be frank, drinking blood is ghastly. I will have to inject them somehow."

None of us says anything. It's impossible. Soleil looks around at our blank gazes and decides to move forward. "I thought we'd work our way back to the Boggletrice Company by transforming the Einsreich we pass along the way. If it works, that is. I will sneak up on one at the edge of town and try to experiment on it. If the injection is successful, we'll move on to the others."

"Oh, Queen Soleil, what if they hurt you? What if you die?"

"I've got my stone, Princess Calysta. I'm stronger than I look. But let us not forget you three must also be brave. You will have to hide while I test the first subject. If it's successful, I'll need your help injecting the others. You have stones too. I am sorry, but you must be brave now, young ones."

Atticus, Calysta, and I all have obsidians in our crowns. But how good are we at using them?

"That's right, I keep forgetting," says Calysta, feeling the blood-red stone above her forehead.

"Blimey, me too," says Atticus standing up straighter. He has never allowed his small stature to dim his courage.

Miss Squaffletree's hand is on her chest, and her brows are furrowed with worry. "Oh dear, I'm a ball of nerves. Do be careful, children. Run back here at any time. The library is your safe haven. Remember that always. You as well, Queen Soleil. If the injection doesn't work, these doors are always open to you."

"Thank you, Miss Squatty. You are too kind to us." And with that, Soleil grabs her black leather bag and the four of us humans and one lumpy dragon are off to Downtown Ipswich.

Chapter 21
Marked

"Is there enough of the golden blood, Soleil?" I ask. "There are hundreds of Einsreich. Maybe thousands by now." I say, remembering the kidnapped children.

"There is enough to get us to the pub. After that, I think I know what I'll do, but I'm still going over it in my mind. If you remember the story, Pippin's power easily brought Brumbletide from the Digglewip. It took Michelle years to build Emily, and he had to slaughter thousands of Snickerlings to do it. In the same way, it probably took loads of warmouth blood to create the Einsreich, but the golden blood just might restore them with only a small amount. Alright, everyone, quiet. Hide over there."

We have reached the Ipswich bridge. Four Einsreich stand guard, two girls on our side of the canal, two boys on the other. Their heads are down, hanging creepily. They do not have any sort of consciousness except to carry out orders from Tritch and Klauschwitz. If they were, in fact, real kids at one time, it really is such a sad situation.

"Don't the people here wonder what the heck these things are and what they're doing here?" asks Atticus. "Why isn't there some kind of commotion?"

"It is strange," says Calysta. "The town seems quieter than ever."

Soleil is too focused on her test subjects to listen to Atticus and Calysta. "I'm going to go under the bridge. Right up there by that girl closest to us. I will carefully crawl up behind her, inject her arm, and jump back under the bridge as quickly as I can.

"Be so careful, Soleil," pleads Calysta.

"I will. You three be ready to run. But if all goes well, I'll come back here, and all of us will restore the others."

I gulp. By "restore the others," she means we'll inject the zombie kids.

Soleil stealthily slips down through shrubs to the water's edge and makes her way under the Ipswich bridge. She climbs up the small mound of earth beneath the end of the bridge to where the Einsreich girl is just above. Atticus, Calysta, and I watch from behind our bush, our hearts pounding so hard I swear we can feel each other's heartbeats. Soleil slowly pokes her crowned head from under the bridge and gets a quick look at her target. Then, before we can blink, she is up on the bridge behind the Einsreich injecting her arm with the syringe of golden blood. Soleil disappears back under the bridge just as quickly. The Einsreich girl didn't flinch!

We watch the girl. Soleil watches us. Nothing happens.

The girl stands stiff as a haunted statue. Her scraggly hair hanging over her white face is the only thing that moves, and only because of the breeze.

Soleil and I make eye contact. I only shrug. Soleil's shoulders fall in disappointment.

But suddenly, Calysta gasps. The Einsreich head lifts, and the stiff body seems to loosen. It steps, almost falls, forward as if breaking out of restraints.

We stare, holding our breath. The girl looks around herself as if she doesn't know where she is but then notices the other Einsreich and is visibly startled. She hurriedly stumbles away and then runs off toward the wood. Mouths hanging, we give Soleil the thumbs up.

Soleil runs back to us. She grabs her bag and talks quickly, filling several syringes with tiny amounts of golden blood. She doles them out to each of us.

"I don't know how many are out there, but this is definitely a time you must be brave, young ones. Act swiftly and use your stone if you find yourself in harm's way."

Atticus, Calysta, and I all have one hand full of small syringes, the other ready to either inject of fight. Once all the syringes are dispersed, Soleil takes a deep breath. "Inject them in the upper arm, thigh, buttocks, or hip. Are you ready, children?

"No," all of us say, even Atticus.

Wow! Finally, not just me!

Soleil smiles, amused. "I understand. I'm afraid you have

to try."

"We've got this, Queen Soleil," says Atticus, back to his usually self.

"That's the spirit, Prince Atticus."

Calysta stretches out her hand, and Atticus does the same, putting his hand over hers. I add mine to the stack. With curiosity and amusement at this, Soleil places her hand on top of the rest of ours. She beams at us kids.

"For the kids at the academy," Atticus whispers.

"Yes, and our families and the people of Little Ip," adds Calysta quietly.

"For Pippin and Brumbletide," I say, surprising myself.

"And for the world," says Soleil, and we quietly raise our hands in triumph. Soleil adored the whole thing.

We carefully step down the rocks, each of us trying to hide behind bushes when available. When we reach the water's edge, we follow it to the bridge.

"Maggie, you take the other girl, and I will oversee Atticus and Calysta as they go for the two boys. All of you be ready to use your stone. The unexpected is always expected. Once these Einsreich are injected, be immediately ready to inject the next."

We all agree and waste no time getting into action. I don't think any of us kids want to give ourselves time to be afraid. Calysta and Atticus climb to their designated Einsreich. Soleil huddles on the earth mound between them. I climb up underneath the other Einsreich girl and try to tell myself that I'm really good at using my stone now. Atticus, Calysta, and I instinctively look to

Soleil for the go-ahead. Her small lips mouth "Go," and everyone swiftly moves to make their injection. Somehow, I follow through with our plan seamlessly. I climb quickly behind the Einsreich—stick, push, remove, and swing back under the bridge. Atticus and Calysta have done the same, and the four of us huddle together, listening and waiting.

Again, nothing for a little while. But after that, we hear voices! A boy's anxious voice speaks what I'm thinking might be German.

"I think I'm going to be sick." That was the Einsreich girl I injected!

"What are we doing here? Who are you?" It's the other boy.

Soleil climbs onto the bridge, and we all follow. The Einsreich have regained their color, but not much. They are no longer zombie-pale but slightly green, like someone ill. All four are completely coherent and have their wits about them. Their eyes are brown and blue, not red. The golden blood really works!

"You are safe, and you must listen to what we have to tell you."

"I don't think the one boy can understand us, Soleil," I say of the one speaking in a foreign language. His forehead wrinkles at my words.

Soleil speaks in English to the boy. "Can you understand me, young man?"

"Ja," he replies.

"He understands me." And Soleil begins to explain to the

Einsreich what is going on.

What just happened?

The girl pukes off the side of the bridge.

"Oh dear," says Soleil.

"We can't leave them like this. They have nowhere to go," says Calysta.

"You're right, Princess. How did I not think of this? They have nowhere to go."

"Well, figuring out that your dragon had died in the blood of a White Stag king and then was resurrected, leaving its blood able to restore zombie children to normal, and then training three thirteen-year-olds to help you inject the zombie kids without causing sudden death tends to take up space in the mind." Atticus takes a deep breath after his stream of words.

"The library. Miss Squaffletree said her doors are always open to us. Surely, she wouldn't turn away sick children," says Calysta.

"That will have to do for now." Soleil turns to the bewildered Einsreich. "Come with us. We'll get you some help."

At first, they seem understandably apprehensive about following us. Still, when they look past the bridge back into Downtown Ipswich and see dozens of eerie, lumbering royals dressed like themselves, they decide we are the better option.

"Good thing Miss Squaffletree is Miss Squaffletree," says Calysta.

The four of us take the four Einsreich (who technically are no longer Einsreich anymore) to the library. Each of them gets sick multiple times on the way.

"Poor things," says Soleil. "It must be the warmouth blood and who-knows-what-else they were infused with that should never enter a human body."

"I-I'm sorry—cough—could someone please tell us a little more—" but the girl erupts into an uncontrollable coughing fit and can't finish her sentence.

"We'll explain everything once you feel a little better. You need rest and nourishment," Soleil explains.

"You don't remember anything about how you, you know, got like that?" I ask.

"Like what?" the English-speaking boy replies curiously.

"Maggie!" Exclaims Calysta. "Shine your light on them!"

I put two fingers on my crown and shine the red light on the girl. Her crown, which was previously cocked to the side, hanging off her zombie-like head, is now poised between two glorious white antlers.

"They have Pippin's mark!" pipes Calysta.

"Whoa," says Atticus, shining his light on them. "Wild! Who would've thought?"

"Oh dear, this is wonderful news, but I believe we are scaring them. Let's keep moving, everyone." Soleil tells us as she guides the anxious Einsreich gently by the shoulders. The three of them have wide, bloodshot eyes—though no red iris—and looks of utter concern.

By the time we get to the library's gate, Atticus, Calysta,

Soleil, and I all have an Einsreich leaning heavily on us for support. Thankfully, their unnaturally large size has diminished with the golden blood injection. Miss Squaffletree runs out the front doors to help. "I was not expecting you all back so soon. Who do we have here?"

"They are, or were, Einsreich, Miss S. The injection worked!" Calysta explains.

Miss Squaffletree gasps examining the two boys and girl. "How wonderful! Are they—are they alright?" she says, noticing their sickly dispositions. The girl has been taken by another coughing fit, and the German boy is puking.

"They need rest and nourishment. We didn't know where else to take them?" explains Soleil.

"Say no more. Come with me, children. But do try to stay quiet. The library is open and has patrons."

The four Einsreich stumble wearily to Miss S. who guides them into the library. "Bring them here if you can heal more. There is plenty of room."

I think back to the hundreds of Einreich in Emily's dungeon and try to imagine them all crowded in the library. It's big, but is it big enough? I decide not to say anything and cross that bridge when we come to it.

"There's more than meets the eye here," Miss Squaffletree adds, eyeing me.

"Many thanks, Miss Squatty. We may see you again soon, but hopefully not before we have reached the Boggletrice Company."

"Godspeed to you all," Miss S. bids us as she closes the door to tend to the Einsreich.

"Alright, back to the task at hand. Everyone got your syringes?" Soleil removes one of hers from her pocket.

"Got 'em," says Atticus, and we all hold ours for her to see.

"Good. Strike quickly. Use your stone when necessary. Let's go."

Atticus, Calysta, and I run after Soleil back to the Ipswich bridge.

Chapter 22
Legends

Swift and determined, we run back to the town. The frigid wind pushes us forward as if this were our purpose from the beginning, and it is carrying us to it. We pause at the bridge that still has no Einsreich standing guard. The ones that were there are real kids again and healing in the Ipswich Library, but there are many more where they came from. Across the bridge, we see Einsreich at almost every window of every shop. They are in the grass and by the benches, under the cherry blossoms and by the lampposts.

Soleil takes out the jar of golden blood from her bag and fills more syringes. "When you run out, come back to me. We don't have to get all of them this time, just enough to make our way back to the Company. Then we can show the others how to help us." She throws her bag over her shoulder. "Are you ready, children?"

"Let's do this," says Atticus.

We're off.

"Your stones! Don't forget!" shouts Soleil.

The four of us ready our syringes and without a word, stab the first Einsreich each of us comes to. Atticus injects one by Yoyo's, Calysta gets one by a bench, Soleil stuns a girl in front of Mr. Peabody's practice, and I easily inject one across from it.

And that was all there was of an easy part.

An Einsreich under a cherry blossom screams before I can inject it. I quickly stab the syringe into its arm, but it's too late. All the other Einsreich are screaming now and lumbering toward us.

"Stones!" yells Soleil, and beams of her white light and our red fly everywhere.

Where are the townspeople? How is no one seeing this?

The beams of light knock back the Einsreich a bit so we can get away, but they don't stay down long. I shoot my beam at a clunky Einsreich boy who has his red irises set on me. His arms are stretched out in front of him as if he is following them where they lead. When I knock him back, Soleil injects him in the arm.

Many of the Einsreich are real again now, coughing, vomiting, and running into the woods screaming in terror.

"Get away from here!" Soleil tells a group of them. "Run and find help for yourselves wherever you can!"

We've come to Mrs. Cloudt's bakery. Lazy Jug is just ahead! Calysta and Atticus blast two Einsreich, and I immediately inject them.

"We're out! We need more syringes!" calls Calysta.

"Hold tight, Princess!" yells Soleil as she blasts three Einsreich at once. She throws me her bag. "Replenish everyone's supply, Maggie!"

I run to Atticus and Calysta blasting two Einsreich along the way. Soleil blasts even more and injects them herself immediately as I open the bag and grab a handful of filled syringes for Atticus and Calysta. I get several more for myself as well.

A white limousine screeches down the cobblestone path of Downtown Ipswich. The black window lowers and Tritch Anguis yells, "Stand down, friends!"

The Einsreich stop pursuing us immediately at Tritch's command.

"Get out of here! We'll attack!" Atticus yells bravely.

"Young man, your time at Emily is over. I will notify your mother at once."

Atticus turns white. Mrs. Peabody has no idea he hasn't been at school.

"You can take your stupid school and shove it—" But Calysta stops as Thorn gets out of the limousine.

"That's it, Thorn. Good girl. Do your duty as Head of Emily."

Thorn is quiet and nervous. "Ma-Maggie, you've got to come with us."

"Come off it. Are you dense?" says Calysta.

"No, Thorn," I say.

"They'll kill me if you don't. They said I have to perform as Head of Castle, or I am not worthy to live."

"He won't kill you. He's your dad." Is Tritch *that* terrible?

Thorn's beady black eyes twinkle with tears. "I-I think he might," she says quietly. "Please come back, Maggie. Please."

"We can't, Thorn!" I tell her in almost a panic. I didn't anticipate this. Is she being truthful?

There is a flash of blue light and a crash. Tritch yells. A flash of yellow light blasts from above, and another of the limousine's windows blows out.

"Where's it coming from?" Tritch yells. "Einsreich, attack!"

But just as the Einsreich come at us again, more yellow light comes beaming down from an upper window of Lazy Jug, and along with it beams of blue, purple, red, and green blast down as well.

The whole front window of the limousine crashes into the driver's lap—the driver we now see is an Einsreich. It screams a shrill, ear-piercing scream that is enough to burst an eardrum. Tritch is yelling something impossible to make out over the noise.

Meanwhile, Soleil, Atticus, Calysta, and I are blasting Einsreich and injecting as many as we can.

"Get in, half-wit!" Tritch yells at Thorn who scurries into the car. They screech out of Downtown Ipswich hitting many benches and lampposts along the way. The spooked Einsreich driver is having a hard time.

Colorful beams continue to flash and blast down from the upper room of Lazy Jug, and soon, the front door flies open.

"Come on, lads!" Gus yells.

He doesn't have to ask anyone twice. We all race into the safety of the pub.

Once we're all in, Gus slams the door, locks all the locks, and puts a chair up against the knob for good measure. The door to the apartment I stayed in when I ran away opens and the Chosen fly down the stairs to us.

"Oh, my dears, you fought valiantly! We are so proud," Eve says, embracing Atticus, Calysta, and me like a mother hen with her chicks.

"All of you fought well," says Justice, "but let's get back to the headquarters where we won't be seen."

"There's no one out there, You're Majesty," Atticus explains as he lines up behind Justice at the fireplace.

"There's a reason for that, lad. We'll explain," says George.

We all file through the fire into the cozy cottage where the rest of the Company eagerly awaits.

Anastasia, Henry, and Cornelius greet us with gasps of relief that we are alright, and Jack and Wes have no shortage of questions. Jericho flies overhead, and Lenore, elegant and poised as ever, is genuinely happy to see us all.

"Everyone, let's calm down and have a seat. Justice, some Bubblegin, please. I've got bread fresh out the oven." Martha holds a pan of bread with mitted hands.

We all gather at the table as Justice pours glass after glass, and Mrs. Cloudt slices the bread. Sara Lisa brings butter and a knife. There is nothing like reuniting with these people after a battle—something I never in a million years thought would become commonplace for me.

Settling down, no one says anything at first to keep some order in the room. When we all have Bubblegin and bread and have caught our breath, Mrs. Cloudt says, "Maggie, you should tell us what you all have been through before we reveal our recent discoveries. You've certainly seen a lot."

"I'll say, Mrs. Cloudt," says Soleil playfully.

"Go on then," urges the baker.

I try to think of where to begin. "Well, it all started when we were caught by Tritch and the Einsreich when returning here from the library."

"Brilliant place. You wouldn't believe the sorcery they have there. Like nothing you've ever seen," Soleil tells the other ancestors.

"Maggie was taken back to Emily," Calysta continues. "I ran home but eventually went to the library. I don't know what made me think of going there, but it just seemed like I should. Soleil and Atticus went looking for the ingredients Soleil needed for the antidote for the Einsreich. Of course, we didn't know where everyone went until we were reunited at the library."

The whole Boggletrice Company shifts to Soleil who blushes sheepishly.

"Soleil," George says in disbelief. "Seriously?"

"It was better to go and ask for forgiveness later than to ask all of you and waste a bunch of time arguing."

With a shake of her head, Sara Lisa says, "Please continue, children."

"Tritch kept close watch on me at Emily. I had to attend

classes just like everyone else and was even made Regina of Firebreather House."

"Wow! Congratulations, Maggie!" exclaims Calysta.

I cock my head to the side.

"Oh, that's right," Calysta says. "Not a good thing. I keep forgetting."

"Tritch said I was only made Regina to keep everyone from asking too many questions and that he would kill me as soon as he could."

"Bless," says Eve, clutching her chest.

"But it wasn't all bad. Queen Mother Stiorri is on our side and helped me as much as she could. And then Ernie came."

"Yes. We sent Ernie with the lady of the library. That was before Calysta made it there," Eve explains. "He said he thought the library woman might be helpful because she had been kind to him when he was small."

Miss Squaffletree is the best.

Flori continues. "No one had seen him with us or you, so it seemed safe to send him, you see."

My throat starts to close with anxiousness. "He—Ernie. He's still in Emily."

Eve holds my hand on the table. "We'll get him out, darling. Don't worry."

I do not tell them I couldn't see the Digglewip. I'm not going to.

"Keep telling us what happened, dear," urges Sara Lisa.

"We had to study and care for these horrid plants called verecundiam—or the Shame Plant."

The whole Boggletrice Company gasps. George smacks the table.

"That's it!" pipes Soleil.

"Of course!" exclaims Justice.

"They're washing their minds!" adds George.

"Shame Plant. A gorgeous creature with highly potent and horrendously vocal leaves," Flori recalls. "In the right hands, it can be used for a lot of good. In the wrong hands, it'll destroy legions."

"There are loads of them, Flori. They're everywhere screaming horrible things to the students. Makes you want to cut your ears off or burn the whole building down. Oh! That reminds me, Firebreather Hall *did* burn! I think someone tried to kill me and ended up burning Firebreather to ashes. Thorn and I were placed in Whitescale Hall while Firebreather was being restored. You will never guess who I met there."

Everyone is still, waiting with bated breath.

"Who?" shouts Flori.

"A ghost named Clair Shelley took me to the dungeon where I spoke to Queen Gemma!"

Everyone stares, mouths agape.

"Are you feeling alright, darling?" asks Eve. She feels my forehead.

"Yes, seems the smoke may have gotten to you a bit," adds Justice.

"Gemma," breathes Gus in wonder.

"It really happened! Clair Shelley lived forty years ago and was killed by Emily. And Gemma did not kill herself. She was murdered by one of the Anguises!"

"Maggie, dear, are you certain? This does not go along with anything we've been told," says Eve.

"That's because she was killed just before she finished her letter. She wasn't going to finish it. She said she would never kill herself. It was Cassian Anguis who killed her and then finished the letter and signed her name."

"That's disgusting!" exclaims Anastasia, the first Horseman to speak yet.

"It does make sense, though," says Henry, much to my surprise. "Makes a lot more sense than Gemma killing herself."

"When McShanihan rescued me from the dungeon the night I killed Julian and Louie, he spoke to some eyes in the wall. Those eyes are Gemma!"

"Well, I'll be," says Gus with a laugh. "That queenie stuck around for such a time as this. Just like her, it is."

"Clair and Gemma think they are memories. Michelle's spirit lives on in those loyal to Emily; they think something lives on in those who hate it too."

"Well, that's confusing," says Sara Lisa.

"And strange," says Justice. "Why would his spirit live on in those who hate him? That can't be right."

"It is very strange, but tell us what else happened," says Eve.

"After I met with Clair and Gemma, Tritch threw me in his chambers to keep a close watch on me. The room was filled to the brim with Shame Plants. I thought I was going to lose my mind, but then Pippin appeared. He didn't say anything or even look at me. Nothing!"

"Sounds right," laughs Flori.

"Then he was gone. And that's when Zelda came."

As if on cue, there is a rumble in the chimney and the white dragon flies into the cottage in a blast of soot. Zelda rolls to the middle of the cottage and sits proudly, wagging her bum.

"She's filthy!" yells Justice, grabbing a towel.

"Aw, that's alright. She's a good girl," Flori says, going over and giving Zelda a good rub. To Justice's horror, Zelda takes flight, shaking off the soot, and flies over me, licking my hair.

"Good girl," I laugh. "You guys wouldn't have believed your eyes. She transformed into another dragon completely. Even scarier than Gabriel!"

"Really?" George says, examining the little, lumpy dragon as if for the first time. "How peculiar."

"Everyone, we have some incredible news. It turns out that Zelda is the Golden Blood Warmouth," Soleil tells everyone, grinning.

"No, you're not serious?" breathes Sara Lisa. "The Golden Blood Warmouth is only a legend."

"Is it true?" asks Eve expectantly.

"Look!" Soleil takes the glass container from her black leather bag that holds Zelda's golden blood. "Behold!"

Everyone—ancestors, Horsemen, Gus, Mrs. Cloudt, Wes, Jack, Lenore, and Jericho—they all gasp at the sight.

"Unbelievable!" exclaims George.

"Believe it!" smirks Soleil.

"And it restores the Einsreich," adds Calysta, beaming.

"What?" everyone breathes in shock.

"Yes. They are very sick afterward, but it heals them of their zombie state," Soleil explains.

"So that means," George takes Zelda's head gently in his hands. "She died in battle that day. Oh, girl, we didn't know. All these years, we had no idea."

"What a good girl," Sara Lisa tells her quietly, stroking her back. "A brave girl."

The jolly dragon soaks up the attention with glee.

"You guys don't understand. She was vicious! Her eyes were fiery, and she blasted fire at Tritch Anguis."

I have never seen George look prouder than he does right now at Zelda, who wags her bum.

Squeak! Magnus squeals jealously.

"Oh, come now. Let her have her moment," Eve tells him.

"Zelda rescued me from Emily and flew me to the library where Calysta was already with Miss Squaffletree. Soleil and Atticus showed up shortly after. When I told them what happened, that's when Soleil figured out that Zelda was the Golden Blood Warmouth. She drew some blood from her and tested it on one of the Einsreich that were standing guard at the Ipswich bridge. It worked, but that girl ran away. When we injected the others, we took them to the library. They are there now."

"In the library?" Justice says with an unsure expression.

"Yes. Miss Squaffletree is taking good care of them. But there's something else," says Calysta.

"Of course," moans Mrs. Cloudt.

"No, it's surprisingly wonderful. I don't know what made me do it, but I shined my light on one of the Einsreich on the way to the library and then on the others. They bear Pippin's mark!"

If expressions made sound, these would be an explosion in the cottage.

"Blimey, Pippin! He's brilliant!" shouts Cornelius.

I don't say anything, but I wonder why he thinks so.

"Don't you see? The Einsreich aren't the enemy. They are victims. And the more we rescue, the more we have on our side!"

"Well, wouldn't ya know," says Gus with a big grin. "That ole Pippin is taking that wicked Tritch's army—"

"And making it his own," Flori says gleefully.

Chapter 23
Boggletrice for Pippin

The tension lifts in the cottage for the moment, and everyone claps and cheers. But, of course, it couldn't last long.

"What now?" Henry's blunt voice is like an out-of-tune piano. "Are we going to go out and inject the creatures? When do we start?" He twitches his bushy black mustache, and his arms are crossed seriously.

I need to remind everyone again. "Ernie is still in Emily. Zelda couldn't rescue both of us."

"It's alright, darling. We'll get him," reminds Eve.

How? It seems like no one is as worried as they should be about Ernie. It makes me crazy that he is all alone at Emily after everything he's been through. And now the Shame Plants will be reminding him of all his demons every five minutes. "He's stuck in there with those awful Shame Plants telling him constantly that he's a murderer. I'm so worried about him."

"All the more reason to get going then," says Henry. "What's the plan?"

Soleil opens her bag at the table and takes out the syringes. "The good news is we have an antidote for the Einsreich. The bad news is I'm running low on syringes. We've got to get some more somehow. The golden blood must be injected into the Einsreich. It's the only way."

"I can help." It's Atticus. "My dad's a doctor. His practice is just a few doors down. He should be there now."

"But he's not," says Gus solemnly.

Atticus raises his brows, giving Gus a side glance.

"Now we'll give ya our bit of knowledge," Gus says gently. He pulls a beautiful envelope out of his vest. It has Emily's purple wax seal on the back. "This here's from Emily. We all got one, all us shop owners here. You want to do the honors, Queenie?" Gus gives me the envelope with the pub's address written in royal calligraphy on the front.

Clearing my throat, I read to the room,

"Dear Royal Majesties of Little Ipswich,

With recent tragic events happening all over England, it is Emily's top priority not only to send aid but also to investigate and solve the matter as quickly as possible."

"Ha! As if Emily could do anything about it. And the fact that *they've done it* is the real ringer!" jests Sara Lisa.

I continue the letter. *"You may be thinking it is unnecessary for Emily to get involved with an issue of such magnitude as the disappearance of thousands of children around*

England and abroad, but as the next generations are our most cherished pursuit, we at Emily cannot stand by and do nothing while our children are in harm's way. And as Little Ipswich is our main domain, we are immediately beginning our work here at home. The castle will be manning the town with our top royals, specially trained for times of distress. We will need one week to place them and get them situated in the town. Please take a week off from running your businesses to allow this, and Emily will compensate you for your lost hours. Your city will be safe when you return to work in one week. Thank you for your patience as we try our best to protect you all.

Sincerely,

Thorn Anguis

Head of Castle"

Lenore laughs sarcastically at Thorn being Head of Castle. I frown at the load of dog doo that is this letter. "Unbelievable! The children are missing because of Emily! Thorn told me she was almost sure her dad was up to it."

"Certainly right, dear," replies Lenore coolly.

"Of course. No surprise there," says Flori, petting Teddy the beaver curled up in her lap.

"Well, this isn't all bad, is it? The people aren't here, just the Einsreich. We know how to cure them!" Atticus explains encouragingly. "We'll just get more syringes from Dad's office and get to it."

Everyone ponders Atticus's words. I can tell that, like me,

they think this plan sounds too easy to work. After a minute, George finally says, "Sounds like a good plan to me."

"Me too," adds Flori.

"Keep in mind it may be a simple plan, but we are still fighting enemies that will certainly fight back," Henry offers.

Something occurs to me. "One good thing is that when you guys were blasting Tritch's windows, he ordered the Einsreich to stand down. They have to do what they are told. So, unless he has ordered them to attack again, they shouldn't mess with us."

"Let's hope that's the case," says Calysta.

Soleil takes another large syringe out of her bag. Zelda slinks away sheepishly. "Oh, I know, girl, but it's for a good cause. This isn't fun for me." Soleil kneels to Zelda who allows her to draw some more golden blood.

"It's beautiful," Anastasia says, watching.

Fergus goes over to Zelda and licks her head sympathetically.

"Has anyone thought about how many Einsreich there are and how much golden blood Zelda has?" asks Atticus. "There were hundreds in the dungeon when we were there. I'm sure there's more now."

"I have," says Soleil, not looking up. "But that's more than I can handle right now."

A heaviness falls on the room as we watch sweet, jolly, funny Zelda give her blood to the large syringe. None of us want to think of how much blood will be required of her or if she can provide enough to heal all the Einsreich—and live.

Soleil pushes the blood into the jar and fills the syringes she has left. "Who's all going with Atticus?"

The three Horsemen, who are all completely human currently, stand up. "Since everyone's gone, I don't see any reason why we can't help," says Cornelius, smiling.

"I guess you're right, sir," Soleil laughs.

Cornelius removes the brown leather bag that holds the Scepter from the hideous creature's mouth. When he takes it out, nervous tension immediately floods my system. I clench my fists and grind my teeth.

"Honestly, why can't *we* go?" Eve asks the Chosen.

"There's no reason why not," says George standing up.

"Atticus, we'll go with you. You'll get the syringes, and we'll all fill them and get down to business," Sara Lisa says.

"That's the spirit, Queen Gran!" pipes Gus. He is a direct descendant of Sara Lisa and Boris. "We'll get the whole Company on this, we will!"

Justice is deep in thought with his arms crossed.

"Justice, are you in?" asks Sara Lisa.

"I am. It just seems like we shouldn't send *everyone* out. Wes and Jack, I know you two have been couped up here for a long time, but could you stay here with Lenore a little longer? You two haven't used your stones as much as everyone else."

"Aw, come on!" groans Wes. Jack puts a hand on Wes's shoulder.

"You too, Jericho?"

"Of course, King Justice. I'm useless in this case."

"And Gus and Martha, would you stay with them too?"

"Aw, come on!" cries Gus.

"We will, Justice," Martha replies.

"Thank you. It's just as important to leave a remnant as it is to go out and fight." Justice turns to the rest of us. "Alright, let's get ready."

The Horsemen grab hold of the Scepter, and light blasts through the room along with wind that knocks over everyone's Bubblegin. In the roar, we can still hear Martha shout, "Dammit, we did it again!"

The light dims, the wind slows, and Henry, Anastasia, and Cornelius are three majestic, royal Horse-people.

"We're ready," says Anastasia, slipping the Scepter back into its leather bag and placing it in the creature's mouth. My shoulders and jaw relax, and I take several deep breaths.

"Let's go, everyone," directs Justice.

"What about the warmouths?" asks Calysta.

"They'll stay here with Zelda for now. They need their rest for when we need them most," Eve explains. Magnus buzzes on her shoulder defiantly. "Fine, little one. Be safe." Magnus nuzzles Eve's nose and then settles on her crown.

"It's times like this when I think we need a secret handshake or something," says Cornelius.

"A what?" asks George, his lip curled.

"Oh!" pipes Soleil. "Kids!" she stretches her hand out toward us.

BOGGLETRICE FOR PIPPIN

Atticus, Calysta, and I smile and stack our hands on hers. The rest of the Boggletrice Company watches us curiously.

"Come on!" Soleil urges.

Eve grins and adds her hand, then Sara Lisa, then Flori. Before long, the whole Company is crowded together, everyone's hand stacked in the center. Jericho flies above the crowd and adds her hand to the middle.

"This time, we'll yell 'Boggletrice!'" Calysta tells Soleil who nods.

"Boggletrice for Pippin," I offer, unable to help myself.

Soleil beams gleefully. "Alright, on the count of three. One, two, three—"

"BOGGLETRICE FOR PIPPIN!"

Brynn Miller, age 12

Chapter 24
The Eighth Door

Gus goes out first even though he isn't going. He checks the pub and the area. When he returns through the fire, he tells us the coast is clear, and only the Einsreich are in the town. "Still as statues, they are. Not one moves."

"Oh, alright, this is always a pain," mutters Henry. We watch uncomfortably as he, Anastasia, and Cornelius contort themselves in unnatural positions to get their horse bodies through the fireplace.

"Is there anything we can do to help?" asks Calysta sympathetically.

"No, just be patient with us," calls Cornelius, huffing and puffing.

When he has finally made it to the other side, it's the Chosen's turn.

"Olly oop!" Sara Lisa says brightly and disappears into the

fire.

"Hold down the fort, you all," Flori tells the animals before stepping in.

Magnus squeaks from Eve's head as they go next, and then everyone else follows one by one.

On purpose, I am last. I wanted to say something to Jack. Something to let him know he is on my mind often. Something to let him know I care for him. I glance at Jack, then at Wes, Gus, Lenore, and Mrs. Cloudt, who all look back expectantly.

"Bye, Jack. I'll miss you," I say with an awkward wave and run through the fireplace. *Ugh!*

Lazy Jug is now filled with a crowd of Horsemen, Chosen, and children. Has there ever been a stranger group in a pub? But my heart leaps to be a part of it.

"Alright, let's try our best to let Atticus get the syringes without causing any ruckus. No need in fighting until we absolutely have to. What is the best way to your father's practice, Prince Atticus? The most inconspicuous way, of course." Justice asks.

Gus answers when he sees that Atticus is unsure. "The back. Eight doors down. You'll pass two alleys."

George steps in. "Alright, Atticus will go first. I'll be right behind him for protection, Soleil with me. The rest of you follow us in single file. Stay quiet and close to the wall."

Atticus stands up straight with his chin up and chest out as George instructs us. Silently, Gus pops the back door open, the one we took to go to the hospital for Dad. He looks this way and that and closes the door again to tell us that Einsreich are at every door.

"Do you have eight syringes, Soleil?" asks George.

Soleil shakes her head. "Only three."

"Alright, give two to me, and you take one. Everyone else, prepare to use your stones to keep them away for now."

"And tickle them! That worked on that one in the dungeon." Sara Lisa reminds us.

"Oh, that's right!" I exclaim. "I forgot all about that. Clair Shelley tickled the Einsreich to get me to Gemma."

"Brilliant," says Eve.

It is time to go to Mr. Peabody's practice. Everyone straightens up, becoming rigid like dogs ready to attack.

"Do not forget, though the enemy controls them, the Einsreich are not the enemy. They bear Pippin's mark! Be as gentle as possible," explains Eve. "Attack only enough to keep yourself from harm."

This gives me anxiety. The memory of Julian and Louie falling dead on the floor of the catacombs flashes before my eyes. I must focus.

"Let's move, men," says George.

"And women," adds Anastasia.

"Whatever, let's go!" Gus opens the door and claps Atticus on the shoulder as he bravely plods forward. George follows with two syringes, Soleil with one, and her black leather bag.

"Eight doors," says George quietly.

The rest of us file out in uniformity behind them. I am

pretty sure George planned for him and Soleil to have the syringes for the first Einsreich we met. If they attacked, they would inject the first three and move on to the others with their stones. But as per usual, this plan did not go according to plan.

It all happened in a whirl. The first two Einsreich didn't budge. Neither did the third. So I think Atticus, George, and Soleil had grown a little overconfident by the fourth that started screaming when they crossed its path. George immediately injected the screaming Einsreich, and the Horsemen kicked the first three when they came at them. They fell to the ground and Eve and Sara Lisa used their stones to hold them off. But the other Einsreich from down the way were now coming. Flori and Justice ran forward, as did Henry, to fight them off. The injected Einsreich was already restored and puking.

Soleil injected an Einsreich boy, and George used the last syringe to inject a girl. After that, they immediately began using their stones to protect Atticus who was now sprinting to the eighth door.

I only have time to see him lift a doormat and remove a key before Calysta and I are approached by screaming red-eyed boys.

"Now!" Calysta yells, and we blast them back with beams of red light. Two more come at us, and we do the same. I see George standing in front of Mr. Peabody's back door, guarding Atticus and Soleil, who are inside, hopefully filling syringes. Beams of red, yellow, purple, blue, and green light are everywhere. Eerie, broken laughter shrieks and squawks through it all. The Horsemen buck and kick with their strong legs. Calysta and I hold our own, but an

Einsreich takes hold of Calysta's arm. She looks at it dead in the eyes and shoots a beam at its head. It falls, seemingly dead.

"No!" Calysta screams and kneels next to it. "Why did I do that? I could have tickled him! Please wake up."

I blast a beam at a girl coming up behind her.

To my surprise, George is now yelling and waving us to Mr. Peabody's back door. What's going on?

"Come on! Come inside, everyone!"

Light beams continue to blast everywhere as we run to the eighth door and into Mr. Peabody's office.

Inside, Soleil is busy filling syringes. Atticus stands with his dad, who is as white as a sheet.

Chapter 25
Blood for Blood

"Atti," Mr. Peabody breathes. "Is this? I mean, I swear you all look like—now you are certainly horses. Or *some* horse..." he mutters and goes to sit down where there is no chair and falls to the floor.

"Oh, dear!" Sara Lisa runs to his aid and helps him up. Mr. Peabody stares at her face the whole time.

"Dad, I would love to explain, but we don't have time. We've got to inject those creepy things out there with that stuff." Atticus indicates Soleil and the golden blood.

"Oh. Alright, son," Mr. Peabody replies, dazed. "How can I help?"

Atticus looks at George. Having your dad ask how he can help fight royal zombie students isn't a conversation you expect.

"Sir, we thank you for the offer, but it's too dangerous," George tells Mr. Peabody as if this is a suitable answer.

"Dangerous! Atticus, you will not be involved in whatever

they are doing. You will stay right here." Mr. Peabody tells his son sternly.

"Dad, it's alright. I was made for this. And look!" Atticus furrows his brows, touches his crown, and knocks Mr. Peabody's wooden eye chart off the wall with a beam of red light. He then gently lifts it back up with the same red beam and hangs it back exactly where it was.

"Wow, Atti! You've really been practicing!" Calysta exclaims with a high five.

"How did? How did you?" Mr. Peabody mutters.

"I'm telling you, I'm trained and ready, Dad."

Mr. Peabody stares at his son in disbelief.

Soleil fills a few more syringes and then swiftly packs up her things. She passes several syringes to all of the Company. "All set! We're ready. Thanks again, Mr. Peabody."

"No problem. But what are they for?"

"Dad, I already told you, but we don't have time to explain it all the way. Long story extremely short, those things out there aren't some Emily military. Well, they are, but they aren't good. They are regular kids who have been messed with. This blood will change them back."

"Blood! Blood from what?"

"A dragon," says Soleil as if it were no big deal.

"Alright now, even if that were possible—a dragon, Atti, come on—that would be highly unsanitary, not to mention unethical."

"That would usually be true, Mr. Peabody. I assure you, in

this case, it is neither unsanitary nor unethical," Soleil explains.

Mr. Peabody looks back and forth between Atticus, the syringes, and the rest of us. "Unbelievable," he says wearily. He slumps and throws his arms as if in defeat. "Just one second, please." He runs to his front window. "I knew something wasn't right. And not just with these kids or whatever they are. I've suspected something was wrong with Emily since that horrible day your dad passed away, Maggie."

I perk up. That's right, Mr. Peabody was playing cards with Dad the night before it happened!

"It was something about that man that wanted to play cards with us out of nowhere. There was something off about him. That's why I declined to play the next night. He was so loud and bothersome. But then that happened to Guy. And when we went to the next Batch, there was the man at the castle in royal robes. He worked there!"

"King Julian, Head of Academy. He poisoned Dad."

Mr. Peabody's mouth drops. "Maggie!"

Justice cuts in. "I know this is all a lot, kind sir, but we really will have to explain in full later. Everyone, line up. We're going out the front this time. Atticus, you stay with your father. It is his wish."

"No!" Atticus shouts. "Dad, please! I'm ready!"

Mr. Peabody holds his furious son around his shoulders as he watches the rest of us line up with syringes in hand. He eyes me and Calysta. He seems to ponder the situation. He shakes his head vigorously, his eyes squeezed shut, fighting some internal battle.

"Ugh, I am so stupid to do this. I don't know why I am. I am a horrible father. Alright, Atticus, but I'm going with you."

"No, it's too dangerous," says Henry. "He has no way of defending himself." Henry is so tall that he talks down to Mr. Peabody without trying.

"I'm going!" Mr. Peabody says sternly, looking up at the Horseman. "Give me some syringes, please." He holds out his hand to Soleil who gives him a handful. Putting them in the pocket of his white coat, he gets in line with Atticus.

George grins. "Two Champions in the family, I see. Like father, like son. Let's go."

"Just inject any of the usual intramuscular sites," Soleil instructs Mr. Peabody as we follow the Horsemen out of the office. "The Einsreich are strong—abnormally strong. If they come at you, tickle it and yell. One of us will help."

"Did you say tickle it?" Mr. Peabody asks, flustered.

"Tickle it, Dad." Atticus squeezes Mr. Peabody's arms as if trying to squeeze belief into him.

Mr. Peabody calms himself and nods determinedly. "No more questions from me. Let's go."

Like soldiers jumping out of a plane, we exit the doctor's office one by one, running into Downtown Ipswich at the Einsreich and injecting them. Beams of light and ominous laughter already fill the area.

Mr. Peabody runs bravely to the first Einsreich he sees, injects it, hides the best he can, and then repeats the sequence over and over as the Boggletrice Company and Chosen blast around him. After a while, there are equal parts zombie royals and real children now seriously ill. Justice gathers them up and shouts, "I know you aren't well, but there is help. Head that way across the bridge. Go until you see the library. Go there and take anyone else like yourselves with you."

Calysta tickles me free from the grasp of an Einsreich boy who clutches my hair. I immediately inject him.

Mr. Peabody screams. One of the Einsreich has grabbed his arm and broken it.

"Dad!" yells Atticus in the middle of blasting two Einsreich. They both fall over a bench.

Cornelius runs to Mr. Peabody, kicks the Einsreich boy away, and pulls Mr. Peabody up and onto his back by his good arm. Mr. Peabody yelps.

"Take him to the library!" yells Justice blasting a whole group of zombie royals back to inject two at once.

The Einsreich in the town are almost all transformed. Just as we are down to ten or so, we hear screeching tires. A van squeals onto the cobblestone street.

"This doesn't look like a good guy, mates. Run!" George calls.

We all begin running in various directions.

"Where?" I shout.

"Follow me!" shouts Justice, running toward the bridge.

"Wait! Everyone, wait!" calls Calysta. "Look!"

The driver of the van is an Einseich boy. The side door has slung open, and what has stepped out is the most horrible sight I think any of us have ever taken in.

"Ernie! Oh, Ernie," Calysta cries.

Ernie stands before us. He is royally dressed and stands about three feet taller and wider than before. His red eyes stare vacantly into nothingness.

Calysta goes to run to him, but I snatch her back. "No! He's dangerous."

"She's right. That van is surely a trap. We have to leave him for now. Everyone, run!" calls George. "Vacate the premises!"

When we begin running, the screeching scream erupts from Ernie, and he charges clunkily after us.

"I'm so sorry, love," says Eve, and blue light blasts from her crown. Ernie is stunned in place. We all run as fast as we can out of Downtown Ipswich.

"We can't let them know where we're going if they're following us," says George. "Let's go this way." We veer left after crossing the bridge and wind through the woods, ensuring we've lost them before returning to the library.

When we finally arrive at the gates of the library, we are surprised to see many restored Einsreich children lying wearily on the lawn, coughing and vomiting. Miss Squaffletree has two in her arms that she is bringing inside when she sees us. "Thank heavens!" she cries.

"Wait a minute, I know this place," says Flori.

"Oh my, look at you all. A sight for sore eyes," says Miss Squaffletree softly so as not to disturb the two sick children in her arms.

Mr. Peabody's arm is in a makeshift sling that was his shirt, and he is busily tending to the ill children, feeling their heads and looking in their mouths.

"Get Mr. Peabody inside," chirps Soleil to Cornelius, "I can take over, sir. You need care, yourself!"

"He wouldn't have it," Cornelius explains. "He wanted to stay out here and help these kids."

"Very good," smiles Soleil, "but we've got it from here. Go with Miss Squatty now, Mr. Peabody."

All of us royals and creatures bring the dozens of Einsreich into the library as Miss Squaffletree directs us to where to lay them. Once everyone is inside and in a bed, couch, armchair, or blanket, Justice helps Miss Squaffletree bring water and cold towels.

"They're burning up," says Mr. Peabody. "We need aspirin."

"I've got that," says Miss Squaffletree, and she runs to get the medicine.

"I've got some too," says Mr. Peabody, taking a small bottle from his coat pocket. "I need to know what has caused this so I can know how to treat them."

"Might as well give him the story now that we'll be here a while," Soleil says, gently stroking an Einreich girl's hair.

Miss Squaffletree returns with the aspirin and tells us that patrons stopped coming to the library shortly after the letters from Emily were delivered. "I thought it seemed slow while you all were here, but then I checked the mail after you left and realized what was happening. No one else came after that."

"Works out well in this case," Justice says, laying a towel on an Einsreich boy's forehead. "I don't know where else we could have sent them."

"Where on earth did they all come from?" asks Mr. Peabody. "Emily?"

"One of the boys we injected from the bridge speaks German, I think," I say. "Others are English but not from around here."

"Great Scott," breathes Mr. Peabody, giving them all another look.

"It's time to give him the rundown," says Atticus.

"Please!" begs Mr. Peabody.

When everyone has finally been tended to and settled in, Justice helps Miss Squaffletree serve refreshments in her office/bedroom/kitchen.

The Horsemen stay in the library with the Einsreich to watch over them and also because they won't fit in room eighteen.

We all find a place on the bed, chaise lounge, chairs, or the floor as Atticus begins explaining to his father how the Einsreich came about.

Justice hands Mr. Peabody a cup of coffee, which he sips immediately. The mug trembles with his trembling hand. His face goes from white to whiter as Atticus's story goes on, and he spills his coffee on his lap when Atticus tells him about us all being locked in the dungeon and that he and Calysta almost didn't make it. Completely ignoring the hot coffee on his pants, he throws his good arm around Atticus. "My boy, oh, my boy! This is an outrage. An atrocity. An absolute scandal!"

"You're telling us," I huff.

Mr. Peabody embraces Atticus as if he will never let go again. A pang of jealousy shoots through me until I feel an arm around me too. It's Eve.

"Oh, Atti, you are such a brave boy. You will never set foot in that school again. To think we've been *paying* those asses to do this to you, and large sums of money at that! I never wanted to send you in the first place. It was your mother who—"

"Dad! It's alright. We're ok, and at least we know now and can fight against it."

Mr. Peabody holds his son's head in his good hand. "I guess you are right son. But I wish you had told me before so I could have helped you."

"Would you have believed him?" Flori asks. "If ya hadn't seen it for yourself?"

Mr. Peabody seems shocked at the question, but after a moment, his expression softens. "I'd like to think so, but probably not."

Flori sips her coffee looking around the room. "I have been here before, I know it. Librarian, how long has this been a library, and was it ever a castle for a great wicked dragon?"

Mr. Peabody laughs. He's the only one.

"Why yes, it was, Queen Flori. This was the castle of the Dragon who was king of Crescent and Fall. He was killed just before the name of the town changed."

"I knew it! This is where it all happened for me." Flori holds up her three-fingered hand. "This is where I stole that man's satchel, and he sliced my fingers clean off."

Mr. Peabody is the only one shocked that Flori tells this story with a smile.

"And it was just outside there where Sheba found me and took me to the real King."

Mr. Peabody hangs on her every word. "And who is that?"

"Who is that?" Flori pipes astonished at his ignorance. "Who else? Pippin, of course!"

"Pippin! The deer from Emily?"

"The great White Stag, King of Brumbletide," Sara Lisa tells him proudly.

"He's real?" asks Mr. Peabody, bewildered.

"Course he's real," Flori replies, exasperated. "Getta loada this guy, will ya?"

"He's real, Dad," says Atticus. "We've seen him. We've even been to Brumbletide! And he's the one who has put us all up to this."

"He's bringing Emily down," says George.

"And he's using us to do it," adds Flori. "He takes the worst of the world and sets 'em doing good."

He's using us to do it. For some reason, Flori's words hit me like an anvil. He takes the worst of the world and sets them to doing good. That's what this has been about, hasn't it? Pippin *could* end it all, himself. He has the power to do it. But he is letting us be the heroes. I wouldn't have ever done anything like what we've done through this adventure if it hadn't been for Pippin choosing me. And he's still saved the day many times! Blimey, I think it's all going to be alright.

"I'll be," says Mr. Peabody. "Wait until your mother hears."

Atticus scrunched his nose. "Let's not tell her just yet."

Mr. Peabody laughs. "Probably a good call."

Calysta sits at the table with George, Sara Lisa, and Flori. Her head is in her hands. "Sorry to change the subject, everyone, but I can't stop thinking about poor Ernie!"

"Is he alright?" asks Miss Squaffletree.

"No. They've made Ernie an Einsreich."

"Oh, dear! Master Ernie!" Miss Squaffletree cries, horrified. "Oh dear, oh dear, what will we do?"

"We've got to find a way to get to him so we can inject him with the golden blood," Soleil says.

Calysta's head falls on her arms. I'm with her. The task seems impossible. Poor Ernie.

"I know, dear Calysta, but there must be a way. We'll save a special syringe just for him."

"And that's the other elephant in the room," I say. "How will we ever have enough golden blood for *all* the Einsreich? Zelda can't possibly give her blood to all of them! And if all of the missing children on the news are destined to become Einsreich, we're doomed."

Soleil says nothing, which is disheartening to everyone. "There's got to be a way," she finally says, leaving no one feeling encouraged.

"Excuse me, if I may grant a suggestion," says Mr. Peabody. "If I've gathered the information correctly, since the warmouth blood-infused children can be cured with the golden blood, one blood countering the other—wouldn't it then be possible that the cured Einsreich's blood would have the same properties as the dragon's?"

Soleil's eyes grow huge. "Maybe! Mr. Peabody, that's a brilliant theory! It's worth a try."

"I'll do everything I can to help," Mr. Peabody replies.

"Fantastic. So, we have an antidote and a possible solution to the golden blood shortage," says Justice. "Now we need a plan of getting to them, and safely if possible."

"Master Atticus, did I hear you telling your father that Emily's dungeons were filled with Einsreich?" Miss Squaffletree asks.

"Yes, ma'am."

Miss S. brightens and begins lighting a lantern. "Ah, I think I have something that might be quite useful. If you all would please follow me."

We all get up and follow Miss Squaffletree to the large room we now know was the Dragon's great hall. The Horsemen are in various areas helping the Einsreich.

"We will return shortly, kind lady and gentlemen. Make yourselves completely at home and use whatever you can find that might prove helpful. And please, read as many books as you like. Times like these are the best times to do so."

The Boggletrice Company follows Miss Squaffletree to a bookshelf under the long staircase. "You are the first to know this secret in centuries. It is best kept under wraps for the safety of everyone. But I have a strong sense the time has come to share it with you." Miss Squaffletree pulls a crimson copy of *Through the Looking Glass*. The title is in gold calligraphy like the names on the doors at Emily. The bookcase moves to the side revealing another staircase. This one is stone and leads downward. Miss Squaffletree holds her lantern up and leads the way down the dark stairway. I am the last in line, and when I step past the bookcase, it closes back on its own.

As we descend the stairs, the air gets cooler and cooler. When we reach the end, there is a long, dark hallway lit only by Miss Squaffletree's small lantern. Magnus lights himself up adding much more light to the empty hallway. We walk and walk and walk. No one says anything to anyone else the whole way, too curious and anxious to know what the secret is. Finally, we come to a stone wall. A dead end.

Miss Squaffletree speaks quietly. "As some of you may know, but most do not, the Dragon, until his death, had an alliance with Michelle. To more easily meet with one another, the Snickerlings were made to build a secret tunnel between the Dragon's castle and Emily. That secret passageway is what we are standing in right now."

Two eyes blink open in the wall. A mouth emerges underneath.

"Gemma!" I exclaim without thinking. "Oh, sorry to yell," I whisper.

"Nice to see you again, Maggie." The eyes look around at the Chosen. "And I have longed to meet you all. I have never given up hope of joining you in Brumbletide one day."

Everyone stares bewildered at the face in wall. "Nice to meet you, Gemma," says Eve finally. "You'll have to excuse our awkwardness. This is quite the surprise."

The face smiles warmly. "I understand. Let's get to what you are here for. On the other side of this wall is the catacombs of Emily. Yes, the Axiom is here, but I warn you not to go near it. It is highly protected."

"We promise we won't, Queen Gemma. We were only going to take a quick look. I am the librarian of Little Ipswich Library. My family has run it for a few centuries now. With the crisis at hand, I thought it would be good to show the ancestors this connection to Emily. Queen Soleil has found an antidote for the Einsreich but is not ready to use it in mass just yet. We only need a quick look to see if we would be able to get to the Einsreich from here. The Chosen believe the more they can restore, the more will be on our side."

"They bear Pippin's mark," Soleil tells Gemma gleefully.

"I see. How wonderful, Queen Soleil. Well done. I, too, think this passageway will aid you in your endeavor. The coast is clear. Stay where you are, and I will open the door." The eyes close, and the wall slides to the side. What we see next is both exciting and utterly terrifying.

The catacombs, as usual, reek of ominousness. Small skeletons are everywhere, and white wings are all over the walls. But the wings no longer gleam because of the presence of the

Einsreich which are crowded like hideous zombie slaves in the vast room of the dead. In the midst of them, like a giant pearl in a pile of trash, is the Axiom. Inside, snow falls around Brumbletide Castle, which is empty—for now.

THE END

Brynn Miller, age 12

Brynn Miller, age 12

Brynn Miller, age 12

Brynn Miller, age 12

www.ingramcontent.com/pod-product-compliance
Lightning Source LLC
LaVergne TN
LVHW041802060526
838201LV00046B/1098